Annie's World

Nancy Smiler Levinson

KENDALL GREEN PUBLICATIONS

Gallaudet University Press
Washington, D.C.

For my mother

With acknowledgments to John M. Goul; Julianna Fjeld; Betty Josewich; Rose Weinberg; Jean Pappas, Santa Monica High School; Jim Watts and the Division of Special Education, Selaco-Downey High School; Eva Brown; Carol Proctor; Dr. Eugene Flaum; and Maurice Berkey.

The author would also like to thank Gallaudet University Press editors, Ivey B. Pittle and Robyn D. Twito, for their wise and thoughtful guidance.

KENDALL GREEN PUBLICATIONS
An imprint of Gallaudet University Press
Washington, D.C. 20002

Library of Congress Cataloging-in-Publication Data
Levinson, Nancy Smiler.
    Annie's world / Nancy Smiler Levinson.
    p.   cm.
    Summary: Annie, who has been nearly deaf since she was seven, must leave her school and be mainstreamed into a public high school, an adjustment which she finds difficult but ultimately not impossible to handle.
    ISBN 0-930323-65-3 : $2.95
    [1. Deaf—Fiction. 2. Physically handicapped—Fiction. 3. Mainstreaming in education—Fiction.] I. Title.
PZ7.L5794An   1990
[Fic]—dc20   89-78320
                                                CIP
                                                AC

CHAPTER ONE

The minute Annie stepped into the house and saw her father's face she suspected that something was wrong. When she glanced toward Gil, she was positive.

Both her father and brother tried to look casual and relaxed, but they couldn't fool her. She was an expert in reading faces.

"Annie," her father said from the worn chair where he sat, "come and sit here." He patted the footstool in front of him.

Annie moved forward slowly and sat down, facing him directly.

"We have something to tell you," he began. He spoke rather than signed. He had never learned sign language as well as Gil or Annie's mother. Annie's mother had died four years ago when Annie was twelve. Annie watched her father's lips carefully.

"What news do you have?" she signed, while at the same time she nervously burst out with the words, pushing the air and sounds from her abdomen through her throat.

"We have to make some..." her father said.

"What?" Annie asked. She had not understood the last part of his sentence. The important part.

"Changes," he repeated carefully.

"Right," Gil nodded, perching himself on the arm of the chair.

Annie leaned forward anxiously.

"Okay, here are the facts." Her father explained slowly. "The airline has been bought by a big corporation, and...letting half the mechanics go. That includes me. I've looked everywhere around here for a job. There's nothing. Nothing."

Annie looked sympathetically at her father. She couldn't imagine what he would do now. What would they all do?

"But I finally found auto mechanic work," her father went on. "Problem is...auto shop...not near Sacramento. It's in San Lucas. I clocked the freeway time. Two hours each way. Too far to drive every day. I'm sorry, Annie. ...no choice. We have to move."

Annie leaped up. "That's impossible!" she cried. "How can I? How can I leave Sandhurst School? What will happen to me? You don't think I can go to a *public* school, do you?"

"Calm down, Annie, please," Gil said, putting his arm around her, then removing it so he could sign. "We've made the best arrangement possible. I'm going to have to change community colleges and look for another part-time job, too."

Annie wriggled away. Angrily her eyes darted back and forth between the two of them. Her father and her brother. Always a team. Always against her. This time they had gone too far. They had plotted something unthinkable behind her back.

"Public school! Move to another city!" she cried. "I can't go to a public school. They don't take just any deaf student. They will never let me in, and that's just fine with me!"

"Yes, they will," her father corrected her. "The school is called Eldorado High School. They have a good mainstreaming program with a resource specialist. They've seen your school records and your latest audiology test results. Gil and I talked to them twice." He held up two fingers.

"You talked to them about *me?*" Annie's eyes smoldered. "Without my knowing?"

Gil ignored her angry questions and added slowly with his hands. "They're ready to accept you. They want to meet you and evaluate you to see where they can place you."

"You had meetings about me?" Annie asked again, still disbelieving. "You lost your job and found a new one? You made plans to sell the house and move? All that behind my back? How could you? How could you play such a dirty trick on me?"

"Did you say we tricked you?" Annie's father asked, glancing at Gil to be sure he heard that right. Then her father told Annie that they hadn't played any tricks behind her back. "You have to believe that," he pleaded. "We didn't know exactly what was going to happen. Why...upset you before?"

"*We! We! We!*" Annie repeated. "That's all you two say around here. And I'm never part of that *we.*"

Annie's father continued explaining, but Annie turned and stalked away.

Gil caught her shoulders and held her tightly.

"Come on!" he insisted. He dropped his arms and signed quickly before she turned away again. "Why can't you give yourself a chance? You have more going for you than you think. Why do you want to hide at a school for the deaf forever and never meet anyone new?"

"I'm comfortable and happy at Sandhurst," she

3

signed in return. "I don't need to meet anyone else. I like my friends here. What kind of person should I become? Someone like you who thinks about nothing but working out at the gym and getting dates?"

"That has nothing to do with this," Gil was quick to respond.

"Yes, it does," Annie answered. "I'm different, in case you forgot!"

"Before Mom died, her last words were about you, Annie," Gil reminded her. "Mom worked hard with you so you could have more chances in your life. She wanted you to go to a regular school some day. She wanted you to take steps into a little wider world."

"I hate the way you bring Mom into conversations like this!" Annie said.

Their father ran his fingers through his hair and sighed deeply. "Stop fighting," he said. "Please. This is hard enough."

For a minute, Annie appreciated the pain that her father must be feeling. But he would manage to get along fine in time. Gil would, too. But what about her?

The *team* was trying to explain more to her, but Annie was already out the front door. A flood of angry tears flowed as she crossed the street. Beneath the anger a far stronger feeling gripped her. Fear.

At Sandhurst, she didn't have to work extra hard to prove that she had a brain and a mind. And feelings. She was as smart as any hearing kid. She knew that. She just didn't feel confident about herself around hearing kids. But she was a top student at her school. Last year, Annie was presented with the school's outstanding student award. A framed photograph of her receiving the trophy hung outside the school director's office. Besides, her friends and

4

teachers liked her for herself. And she was so close with Kay, sometimes Annie joked that they were twins in another life.

Now Annie, who was almost seventeen, had just started her junior year. How could she be expected to leave Sandhurst and a friend like Kay, move to a strange city, and go to a public school! A public school meant harder work and new subjects. It meant throngs of new people who didn't understand anything about her. It meant being more alone and left out than ever. It meant being a freak.

There had to be some way to get out of going. If only she could live at Kay's house. But Kay already slept in a room with her two sisters. Their whole house was cramped. Maybe she could get a job and earn enough money to pay for a room somewhere nearby. But who would hire her? And what could she do anyway? Type and cook. She considered herself good at nursing skills. A First Aid instructor had complimented her on having a natural touch and good common sense, too. But none of it added up to anything that would mean a reasonable job. It was useless to think there was a way to stay here.

Annie headed for the bus stop on the corner of California Avenue so she could go directly to Kay's house. It was the only way they could communicate. Annie could speak almost normally because she had been hearing until the age of seven. That was when she lost much of her hearing after a bout with meningitis. She also had received a great deal of attention and help from her mother, and was able to wear two hearing aids. Annie was sometimes self-conscious about speaking, though, especially around people she didn't know. She could speechread somewhat but often got flustered and had a hard time concentrating on the person's lips. Her friend Kay was born severely deaf, and oral communication was hard for her. Since Annie and Kay had met at the Sandhurst School for the Deaf, they always signed to each other.

Wait until Kay hears the news! Annie thought.

Just as Annie saw the bus in the distance, an ambulance overtook it. Quickly she turned off her hearing aids to avoid the discomfort that the screech of a siren caused her. After the ambulance passed, she turned them back on and boarded the bus, where she took a seat alone at the back. She didn't want anyone to see her crying.

At Kay's house, she rang the bell several times. There was no answer. She pounded on the door. Nothing. She started pounding again, this time furiously, with both fists. During her first deaf year or two, she used to beat her hands and sometimes even her head against the wall. That was when the frustration had become more than she could bear.

At last, Annie walked around the house and peeked inside the back window. Kay was in the kitchen, and she sensed that someone was outside. She dashed to the door to let Annie in.

The minute she saw Annie she signed, "What's wrong? Tell me. What's wrong?" Kay flashed her hands frantically in Annie's face.

"Terrible, nightmare news," Annie answered with her hands, and she went on signing to tell Kay what she knew so far, sobbing the whole time.

Kay pleaded, "Don't leave me, Annie," while deep, wrenching sobs broke out of her throat, too.

Annie and Kay clung to each other. Annie could hardly begin to comfort herself, so how could she comfort someone else? But she had to make an effort. Kay was trembling.

"It'll be okay, I promise," Annie broke away from her friend and signed as calmly as she could. Then something important came to her mind. *Why didn't I think of it before?* she wondered. "It probably won't work out at all," she signed slowly to Kay, relieved by the sudden new idea. "The high school said I can start there, but they'll see that I won't be able to make it. So they'll make me leave. Kick me right out. Then I'll have to come back here. My dad will have to make arrangements for me. So don't worry, Kay."

"Promise?" Kay asked.

"Promise," Annie signed back, desperately trying to smile through her tears.

CHAPTER TWO

The rain splashed against the window. It seemed like the kind of rain that would go on for a long time before the sun would shine again. *How fitting this dark, gloomy weather is,* Annie thought as she sat at her classroom computer. It was her last day at Sandhurst. Everything was packed. Her father and Gil were coming after school to pick her up. At three o'clock, they would be on the way to San Lucas. What could be darker and gloomier?

Annie ejected her floppy disk from the disk drive and snapped the computer switch off. Seconds later, Mr. Silver stood over her, frowning.

"Why did you turn this off?" he signed. "You didn't finish the lesson."

"It doesn't matter any more," she answered, dropping her hands sharply into her lap after she finished signing.

"Is that what you really think?" he signed, raising an eyebrow. "It doesn't matter any more?" That was always the way Mr. Silver responded. He never preached. He just asked a question. It never failed to make you think about what you had said.

But his method didn't work with Annie this time.

She nodded *yes*. She meant what she had said. It doesn't matter any more.

"Are you *sure?*" Mr. Silver asked, his hand lingering on the last word.

"Yes. I don't have to turn in this lesson. I don't have to get grades here any more...."

"Have I been that bad a teacher?" Mr. Silver asked.

He was acting his clever self again, but Annie didn't understand exactly what he was getting at. "What do you mean?" she asked.

"I must have been a bad teacher for you," he repeated, sighing heavily. "I've spent all these years trying to get across to students that everything matters in one way or another. If Plan A doesn't work, somewhere there's a Plan B. I thought I was honest and clear about that. Guess I wasn't."

So that's the psychology he was using on her. Annie had to admit that it did work, after all. She cared for Mr. Silver so much and had learned so much from him that she couldn't act ungrateful. She didn't want any bad feelings between them. Certainly not today.

"You have been a wonderful teacher," she said and held her hands over her heart.

Mr. Silver smiled warmly.

Paul, who worked at the computer next to Annie's, sat watching them. Mr. Silver turned, poked Paul's shoulder, and signed, "Keep your eyes to yourself, young man."

Then, Mr. Silver stooped down to the level of Annie's chair and looked at her with genuine concern. "You have been a wonderful student," he told her. "I'll miss you. I'll miss your bright eager face and that happy grin when you catch onto an idea or you figure something out."

Annie lowered her eyes. He knew that she had only been pretending that the lesson didn't matter. He knew that she was full of fear at the uncertainty of what lay ahead for her.

"But I won't miss watching you put on lipstick in the middle of class everyday." Mr. Silver laughed and winked before standing again and returning to the front of the room.

Running her fingers lightly over her lips, glossed with a new pink shade, Annie watched the rain a while longer, then glanced slowly around the room. Twelve other kids she had known for a long time were seated with her at tables placed in a large square so that they faced one another. Some kind of communication was always going on that way.

She knew that the next time she sat in school, she would sit in a row with only someone's back to watch. No face or eyes that could say something to her. How could she make Plan B out of that?

All around the room hung posters and pictures and important information. Mr. Silver didn't miss a chance to teach or to make them think. A world map and a California map—both full of magic marker scratches and scribbles—the Bill of Rights of the U.S. Constitution, a list of members of Congress, and a chart of the human body lined one wall of the classroom. There were sayings and brain-teaser puzzles and movie posters. And Mr. Silver kept a bulletin board of newspaper articles about deaf people. One article was about a deaf actor who played a role on a new TV series. Next to that article hung a letter to the editor that criticized producers for hiring hearing people to play deaf characters when there were so many really good deaf actors in Hollywood.

Mr. Silver gave extra credit to anyone who wrote a

letter to the editor of the local newspaper. Annie had always meant to do that, but she had never gotten around to it. She was sorry about it now. It was too late.

Kay sat across from Annie. She wasn't concentrating any more either. She had told Annie that she wanted to skip school on Annie's last day. She didn't want to say good-bye. She had said she couldn't bear it. But Kay was in school after all. She looked as glum as the gray day outside.

The hands of the wall clock skipped forward. In the past, Annie had thought that the minute hand never moved fast enough during last period. But today it seemed to fly. Then the red light over the clock flashed. Class was over. The school day was over. So was her life at Sandhurst. *At least for now,* she reminded herself.

Usually, everyone rushed out of the room at three o'clock. Today they gathered around Annie to say good-bye and good luck. One girl, Jill, presented Annie with a package wrapped in foil paper.

"This is from all of us," Jill signed, gesturing to the entire group.

Annie tore off the paper and found a big caramel-colored teddy bear wearing a white shirt with a tiny red heart and a message: Hug Me. She blinked back a tear, held the bear close, and murmured, "Thank you."

"We wanted to get you a Rolls Royce," Paul joked, fingerspelling the name of the car. "But we changed our minds at the last minute."

Annie laughed.

Another friend, Stephanie, gave the bear an affectionate poke in the stomach. "When you feel lonely, hug this furry guy and think about us," she signed.

Annie blinked again, but it didn't help hold back a flow of tears.

Everyone said good-bye once more, and one by one Annie's classmates left. Kay remained. She gave Annie a small bouquet of flowers and signed, "Forget-me-nots. I went to three flower shops to find them."

At that moment the director, Miss Ross, dashed into the room.

"I wanted to wish you all the best in the world," Miss Ross signed in the rather stiff manner that was her way. "It will take time, but I know you'll make it. All of us feel that way. And I want you to have this." She handed Annie the framed photograph that had hung on the wall outside her office.

Behind Miss Ross and Mr. Silver, Annie saw Gil and her father coming down the hall for her. Gil stopped to shake out the umbrella he carried. When they came into the classroom, they all said good-bye to each other. After Annie's father had thanked the staff many times over, he turned to Annie and said, "We'd better get going now. The freeway traffic will be terrible in this weather."

Annie and Kay put their arms around each other and stood for a long time. Afterward, Annie made Kay promise to ask her parents if they would let her take the bus to San Lucas for a weekend visit. Kay said she would beg until they said *yes.*

Annie followed her father and Gil outside to the car. A U-Haul was attached to it. Annie climbed into the back seat. A few minutes later, they were on the road, heading away from her home and her school. Annie watched the rain spatter on the windows. She put her arms around the bear and hugged it tightly.

CHAPTER THREE

How did Dad and Gil think they could move from a house to a small apartment? Annie wondered. Nothing fit. The living room was so small, her father's comfortable wing chair and footstool were almost on top of the sofa. Gil wanted to sell the chair, but their father refused to part with it. In the kitchen, the refrigerator door could only be opened part way, or it would hit the edge of the table. And, worst of all, when Annie stood in the middle of her new bedroom and spread her arms, she could almost touch the walls. The dull eggshell walls.

The apartment house manager had promised to paint all the rooms and clean the carpets. But he hadn't done anything. He gave her father some excuse. Annie didn't know what the excuse was. She didn't even want to know. Dull walls and ugly shag carpeting were fitting because everything about this place was wrong. Everything.

Annie yanked the terry towel from her head and shook out her long hair. She reached for her hair dryer and brush and searched for an electric outlet to plug in the dryer cord. She couldn't dry her hair in the bathroom because Gil was in the shower. At last she found an outlet, but she had to move her dresser to get to it. And the cord barely stretched to allow her to stand in front of her dresser mirror.

She wouldn't rush blow-drying her hair today. Annie wanted to be sure her hair was full. Her hearing aids had to be completely covered. She was scheduled to meet with the resource teacher at Eldorado at three forty-five. Probably the school would be empty of students by then. But it was possible that she might run into one or two. And if one person found out she was deaf, it would be all over the school by the next morning when she was supposed to start. No one would understand. They would consider her a dummy, and probably some of the students would mimic her as well.

She remembered the time Gil had urged her to join a crafts group at the park. She had been eleven then. Some girl had banged two wooden blocks behind her back. Annie didn't hear the bang, of course. So the girl and her friends had gotten a good laugh. Annie had run out and refused to return.

Annie had decided that it would be best to fade into the school background—simply not let anyone know she was even there. She had written a long letter to Kay and told her about this decision, warning her not to let Mr. Silver know.

Gil swung the door open and burst into the room. He did this often and it always annoyed Annie. She never had privacy. Not even in her own bedroom. Most of the time she couldn't hear a knock. She'd asked Gil and her father to flick the lights when they came in. But a lot of the time, they forgot.

Once she had rigged up a loud bell at the bottom of the door. The next day Gil forgot it was there, fell over it, and chipped a front tooth. That had ended that!

"Mirror, mirror, on the wall…" Gil began chanting. "……………"

Annie's hearing aids were on the dresser top. Gil's mirror image was backwards, so she was unable to catch the rest of his words.

She turned and asked, "What?"

"…how could a sour puss be fairest of all?" Gil repeated and signed. "If you go around school looking like that, who'll want to make friends with you?"

Annie slammed the hair dryer down. "Who would want to make friends with me, anyway?" she snapped, glaring at Gil.

"It's a big school," Gil signed. "You can find some friends if you really want to." He plopped himself across her bed.

"Get off my bedspread!" Annie shouted, giving him a push. "I just ironed this. Don't mess it."

"Stop changing the subject," Gil said, refusing to get off. "In that mirror, I see a pretty girl. Too bad you can't see her, too. Some of the girls I know would kill to have those green eyes and that cute little nose. And a guy I knew once asked me if you went out on dates."

"Cut it out, Gil," Annie signed emphatically. "I'm not in the mood for your teasing."

"Teasing? Why do you always think my help is teasing?"

"Because it is, and I don't need to be rescued."

"Sorry," Gil apologized. "I don't mean that kind of help. You know I only mean helpful help." He slid off the bed and shuffled out.

Annie shrugged. She wondered if there were any truth to what her brother had said a minute ago. Were his friends really interested in her? Did he talk about his sister with them? Did some girl comment on her looks or some boy actually say he wanted to take her out?

With the hair dryer in her hand again, she studied herself in the mirror. For a minute, she practiced smiling. Next she tried out some regular, casual faces. The relaxed smiles and the casual faces were what she needed at school so no one would suspect that she was different. She wanted her face to blend in with all the others.

Then, Annie felt the tiny gold half-moon hanging on a thin chain around her neck. Her mother had given it to her, and she never took it off. She liked to roll it between her thumb and index finger because it felt smooth and cool.

She finished drying her hair, brushed it out, and put in her hearing aids. After that, she applied a bright new plum-colored lipstick. Next she put on her jeans, high-top sneakers, and a white sweatshirt decorated with a cluster of black buttons on the front and down one sleeve. Kay had bought the same sweatshirt on one of their Saturday jaunts at the mall. Annie had a feeling that Kay was wearing hers, too, that very moment.

Finally, she went to find Gil to tell him that she was ready. Her father had hoped to be home in time to take her, but he had called and apologized for being delayed at the auto shop.

As they were leaving the apartment, Gil turned to Annie and signed, "I'm letting you know now I'm just dropping you off. I'm not coming in with you. I have something important to do."

"What!" Annie shrieked. "How could you do that to me! You're probably just going looking for a gym so you can work out."

"I do want to find one around here, but that's not

what I'm planning for today," Gil said. "Go ahead and hate me, but I think you have to go it alone. The time for you to start on your own is right now."

"Please," she begged. "Please come with me. Just this time."

Gil put his arm around her shoulder, gave it a quick squeeze, and turned and headed out the apartment door.

Annie ran down the hall after him, hoping he would change his mind. Hoping that this time he *was* teasing. But when she climbed into the car next to him, she could tell that he meant it. They drove to the school in silence.

In front of the building, Gil kept the motor running. Annie pleaded once more, using her big green eyes this time. But Gil kept both hands on the wheel and refused to move. *He is mean*, Annie thought. *I do hate him right now!*

"I don't even know where I'm supposed to go," Annie said.

Gil let go of the wheel and told Annie to go to a small corner room inside the main office. "It's straight down the hall, on the left. You'll find it right away. There's a sign over the door that says Office. The person you're meeting is Ms. Gordon." He fingerspelled the name, making sure she understood.

Defeated, she slowly pushed open the car door and found herself standing on the sidewalk in front of Eldorado High School. It was huge. The whole building loomed over her. It looked as if it were going to swallow her. She turned to see if Gil were still there, but he was gone. The car had pulled away and was disappearing around the corner.

Suddenly, Annie felt lightheaded. What if she fainted? What if she died from lack of oxygen? She looked for something to sit on so she could lower her head the way she had learned in the Red Cross course. No bench—not even a rock. Only the curb. She sat on the curb for a minute with her head between her knees. But she began to worry that someone might come along and see her sitting on the curb like a child. Carefully she lifted her head, stood, and glanced around. Fortunately no one had seen her.

Annie checked her watch. It was already past the appointment time. What choice did she have now? She had to start this school. Of course, as she had told Kay, that didn't mean finishing. She moved slowly until she reached the door. With a trembling arm she pulled it open and stepped inside. Her legs were heavy. Her feet felt as if weights were tied to them.

She stood in the hall and stared into the empty, cavern-like space. The walls were lined with steel gray lockers. One by one she passed them, reading the numbers—126, 127, 128....

When she looked up, she was surprised to see two students. A boy and girl were talking and laughing as they walked toward her. They wore tennis whites with large shirt patches that said Eldorado Tennis Team. The boy was deeply tanned and had a wide grin that crinkled the edges of his mouth. The girl was blond and had the most perfect posture Annie had ever seen. She had a pair of large round sunglasses perched on top of her head.

As they passed Annie, the boy glanced at her. Instantly, the girl tucked her arm in the boy's and pulled him toward her.

In the morning, the whole school would be full of kids like that—friends talking and laughing, boys and girls with their arms around each other. Annie leaned against one of the lockers for a minute before going on.

Finally, she found herself in front of the double glass doors of the office. Taped on one of the doors was a poster:

ROCK-A-THON!

Rock for Dollars!

HELP the HOMELESS

OCT. 9

Beginning at 7PM - All Night

Sign up Now! (or until you drop!)

Chairperson: Elizabeth "Bets" Fellendorf

Suddenly, someone inside the office opened the door. Annie was startled. The woman said something to Annie, but Annie didn't understand. She panicked. This was the start of days and weeks of nodding and pretending. *Relax and smile*, Annie reminded herself. She had faked it before. She could do it again.

The woman now seemed to be asking her a question. Annie had to take a guess. The question probably had something to do with helping her find her way.

"Ms. Gordon, please," Annie said.

The woman pointed to a corner office. Annie had guessed right. Through the glass door, she saw someone sitting at a desk. A young woman. As Annie approached, she pressed the half-moon against her skin. She stepped into the office and took the chair offered her.

"You must be Annie Meredith," Ms. Gordon spoke and signed at the same time. "I'm glad to meet you." Her signing was graceful, and it reminded Annie of how her mother signed. She reached across her desk and offered Annie her hand.

Annie wiped her clammy hand on her jeans before holding it out in return. Ms. Gordon's handshake was warm.

"I know you must be nervous," Ms. Gordon said. "I don't blame you. I would be. This is my first year in the school district, too."

At least this resource teacher understands something about feelings, Annie thought.

"I want you to know that I'm here to help you," Ms. Gordon continued signing and speaking. "That means for everything and anything. I realize you'll have to take small steps. No one will push you. If someone does, let me know so we can straighten it out. A lot is up to you too, though. ...is very important. Do you understand?"

Annie nodded, even though she hadn't caught the word. Her face must have showed her puzzlement, though. Ms. Gordon grabbed a scratch paper, wrote *attitude,* and then explained it. She also gave an example of good and bad attitudes.

Of course, Annie understood what *attitude* meant. She just hadn't caught Ms. Gordon's sign.

"Your dad.....you...good...oral communication, too," said Ms. Gordon, speaking without her hands this time.

Annie wondered if the teacher were testing her speechreading ability. For a minute, she considered pretending that she had missed the whole sentence instead of only part, which was often the case with speechreading. She could pretend she was terrible at both speechreading and speaking. Then maybe she wouldn't even have to *start* Eldorado at all. But she could tell that Ms. Gordon wasn't going to let her go that easily. She was a young teacher just beginning her job, and obviously she was eager to make everything work smoothly.

"I'm okay at oral communication," Annie spoke. "Average, maybe."

"Annie, your speech is very good," Ms. Gordon exclaimed. "But we can sign during our resource tutoring time every afternoon. Of course, you'll have to speechread your teachers.... don't know sign language.... meeting with several to explain the special needs of mainstreamed students."

Ms. Gordon paused. *Is she waiting for me to say something?* Annie wondered. *Maybe it's my turn to ask a question. But which one? I have so many.*

"Are there other deaf students at Eldorado?" she signed at last, selecting one of the most immediate questions.

Ms. Gordon shook her head. "Not at the moment," she answered, returning to signing and speaking. "We are talking to two families, though. One is considering enrolling a boy. And we are planning to evaluate a girl next semester."

Annie scuffed her sneakers on the floor under the chair. *I'm the first one. The only one. I'm some kind of a guinea pig,* she thought.

"I guess you have many questions," Ms. Gordon said. "Don't worry. We'll get to them in time. Meanwhile I would like to give you a short exam...."

"Exam?" Annie wondered why.

"To find out some things about your feelings, and a little bit about your general knowledge. It will help me fit you into the classes that will be best for you."

No one had told her about an exam. Had her father and Gil known about this?

"Will you give this a grade?" Annie asked. "Does it count?"

Ms. Gordon reached across her desk and patted Annie's arm. "Don't worry," she said. "There's no grade. And no red pencil marks." Then she gave Annie several pieces of paper that were stapled together, as well as a clipboard and a sharp pencil with an eraser.

"Take all the time you want," she smiled. "I'll leave you alone for a while so I won't make you nervous. If you have trouble with any part, just put an X on the number."

She offered Annie a glass of water and then slipped out of the room.

Annie was left to answer several questions involving her background and interests. She hastily scrawled under *Interests* that she liked being with her friends at Sandhurst, shopping and color coordinating, and ice skating. The questionnaire seemed foolish to Annie. Hadn't her family had those secret meetings? Hadn't they already revealed her personal life to a stranger when she didn't know anything about what was happening?

The second page asked that she rate herself on the general level of her mood and her self-worth, and abilities to get along with others and to concentrate on learning. This seemed unnecessary, too, and she quickly indicated herself average in all the categories listed.

Next, she did a few math problems, multiplying and dividing fractions, and working a medium-hard algebra word problem. Then she answered a page of science multiple-choice questions, guessing on about half, since Ms. Gordon said the exam didn't count. After that, she answered some ridiculously easy questions on the name of the current U.S. president, the parts of Congress, and the location of the national and California state capitals. She had a general idea of how a bill became a law, but she couldn't list the steps. She got only six of the seven continents. But when she stopped struggling for the last name, it came to her—Antarctica. Happily she filled it in. She X-ed out a section about folktales and fables. But she knew the titles of several Shakespeare plays, although she hadn't read them. Finally, when asked to indicate her reading preferences, she wrote horse stories, especially *Ride with the Wind,* and romances.

After the resource teacher spent several minutes reviewing the questionnaire and exam, she took a file card from her desk, wrote on it, and handed Annie her class schedule: Homeroom 200; P.E.; Beginning Biology; Driver's Ed; Art. And of course, resource two periods every afternoon. Ms. Gordon explained that, for this semester, Annie would study English and Math during resource.

"We'll start you comfortably and easy," Ms. Gordon signed. "Come. I'll show you around."

Annie followed Ms. Gordon to her newly assigned locker, her homeroom, the gym, the rest rooms, the nurse's office, and the cafeteria, as well as an outdoor eating patio. The cafeteria was enormous. So were the patio and the adjoining lawn.

Next, they went into the biology room. Ms. Gordon told Annie that the teacher, Mr. Tillis, was also teaching driver's ed this year. The room was the size of three Sandhurst rooms. Each high, black-topped table had a microscope on it and was surrounded by four stools. At the back were counters and sinks. A shelf was filled with plastic models of ears and eyes. There were jars packed with frogs and other creatures that were a mystery to her. In a corner hung a full skeleton on a stand. Not a poster. A real skeleton.

Sensing that someone else was in the room besides the two of them, Annie spun around. A man with a beard and bushy mustache had entered the room. He said something to Ms. Gordon. The mustache covered part of his mouth and his face barely moved when he spoke. His eyes didn't show much expression either. Could she speechread this man at all? Through the hearing aids, Annie heard only the low hum of a droning voice.

And she was going to have this teacher for two classes! Should she tell Ms. Gordon that this was a problem already? No, she would find out soon enough how many problems there would be for Annie.

Mr. Tillis shoved his hands in his pockets and restlessly shifted his weight from one foot to the other while he spoke to Ms. Gordon.

"...one reason...starting her slow," Annie understood Ms. Gordon saying to him. Then she said something else that Annie thought was a mistake. "...better...in tenth grade with...."

Annie gasped. Were they putting her, a junior, back into the tenth grade with fifteen-year-olds? Frantically, she signed the question to the resource teacher.

"Yes," Ms. Gordon answered with a smile, as if everything were fine. "It would be wrong and harmful to push you. It's really the best way for you to begin."

Annie looked away, humiliated.

CHAPTER FOUR

The crowds and blur of noise the next morning were overwhelming. Throngs of students passed in every direction, talking, laughing, opening and closing locker doors. Everyone seemed to know each other. Everyone belonged. Annie felt as if she were looking at this new world from the inside of one of those murky, glass biology jars in the science room.

She stood a few feet away from the door marked 200. Did she dare to go in? Before Annie could take a step, a broad-shouldered boy in a hurry knocked against her and threw her off balance. He didn't even stop to excuse himself.

A shrill bell rang. The sound was piercing, but Annie didn't turn off her hearing aids because she didn't want anyone to see her.

Little by little the crowds broke up, and Annie found herself moving with the stream of traffic into the classroom. But where was she supposed to go? What did people do in homeroom? What if she sat at a desk that belonged to someone else?

A girl seemed to be approaching Annie. She wore a hoop earring on one ear only, and a pencil behind the other ear. Annie swallowed and shifted her notebook from one arm to another.

"Hello...new girl...?" she asked.

It was too noisy to catch the whole question, but Annie speechread enough to get the message. She nodded. In her mind she felt Gil poking her and telling her to go on and say something. *It's always so easy for him*, she thought.

"...join...for the...over...."

Annie strained to pick up as many words as possible. It was always hard getting used to speechreading an unfamiliar person. Besides, this person was talking awfully fast. On the other hand, if Annie didn't tell her to slow down and keep her face forward, how could the girl know? But it was a risk to say anything. A risk not worth taking. The girl probably would back off as soon as she found out that Annie was deaf. Most hearing people did. They never knew what to say or do after that.

"...hope you join.... meet...the most...."

The girl wanted Annie to join some kind of group or club? Was that it? It seemed foolish. Annie shrugged. Let this girl think Annie was cold or stuckup or whatever she wanted. It was better than her thinking Annie was a dummy.

Just then the homeroom teacher came in.

The girl turned from Annie and went to her seat.

"...maybe later...after.... you would like...fun...." the girl said quickly and went to her desk.

The teacher saw Annie hesitating. She made a big show of welcoming Annie and directing her to an empty seat. She also made a big show of exaggerating her lip movements.

"I have an announcement," the homeroom teacher said when everyone seemed to have settled down. "We have a program...school district...handicapped students...deaf, blind, one...wheelchair.... open worlds to...special students...."

Annie braced herself. She was not prepared for *this*.

"...happy to have...with...Annie Meredith... with...hearing...." The teacher was pointing to her, explaining that she was deaf and wore two hearing aids. She even went so far as to say that Annie might show the hearing aids to the class sometime because they were extremely interesting.

Annie was mortified. How dare this teacher do such a thing? Annie's gut feeling told her to rush out of there and never come back. She had a good reason for doing so, and no one at home could argue that. She was almost seventeen, too, and it was legal to quit school. But what would she do after that? Where would she go?

Then Annie realized that nothing more was happening. Everyone had looked at her once to satisfy their curiosity. Now the class was paying attention to a boy with a shaved head, who had come in late. The teacher made some homeroom announcements, something about rules for an essay contest or some kind of contest that required writing, and something about stopping cheating, a get-tough policy or program.

All of a sudden Annie felt a tap on her shoulder. The girl next to her handed her a folded note. Annie looked at her, waiting to find out to whom she was supposed to pass it. But the girl tapped the note until Annie noticed that her name was written on it. What an odd surprise! Stiffly, she turned and peeked behind her. The girl with the earring and pencil was grinning at her.

Annie hesitated to open the note right away. What if she were caught and singled out again? Anyway, what could a note possibly say to her? Finally, when the teacher turned to write on the blackboard, Annie opened the piece of paper. The ink was smeared from her perspiration. It read:

> Oops! Sorry, didn't know you were deaf. I was asking you to sign up for the Rock-a-thon. I'm in charge and trying to get everyone to sign up and get pledges for dancing by the hour.
> It's going to be great!
>
> Elizabeth "Bets"
>
> P.S.
> I'm pres. of the politics club, too. I don't know if you can hear talks or anything like that. But you can come. We have open membership. Dues only 50¢ a week and bring an interesting newspaper article. It's really important to keep up on all this stuff going on in the world!!!

Annie hadn't learned to dance. They'd had a few dances at Sandhurst, but she hadn't gone. Dancing was part of the hearing world she wasn't sure she wanted to belong to. She couldn't keep up with news all over the world or anywhere—it was hard, and it took a lot of time. It seemed as if this Elizabeth, "Bets," with the fancy "s" just went around signing up everybody for everything.

Annie crumpled the note and dropped it in a trash basket on the way out. She didn't care if Bets saw her do it. Annie hadn't had a hearing friend for so many years, she didn't know how to act with one. Wait until she wrote Kay about this incident! Kay didn't know how truly lucky she was to be at Sandhurst.

Annie started for the gym. She was sure she remembered where it was. She went down to the first floor and walked all the way to the end of the north wing—but no gym. She refused to ask anyone. She would find it by herself. And if she didn't, missing P.E. was fine with her.

Was the girls' gym in the basement or at the other end of this hall? This was odd. She usually didn't lose her sense of direction. Maybe it was the basement. When she reached the foot of the stairs she was confronted by a girl who reminded her of the broad-shouldered boy who had nearly knocked her over earlier.

"What...you...doing?" the girl asked.

Annie glared at her. What right did she have to stop her like an army sergeant and question her? Annie refused to answer and started forward, but the girl grabbed her arm. Annie snatched her arm away. The girl shouted something about passing or past.

Annie didn't know what she meant. She wanted to reach out and shove her or shake her. Tears of frustration came to Annie's eyes, and she ran up the stairs and down the south hall until at last she found the gym.

Annie changed quickly into her P.E. clothes and entered the gym. The class had already started. Everyone was doing some kind of odd dance movement. A minute later she realized that the whole class had slowed down. Of course. They were staring at her.

The teacher, in black tights and a tank top, was swinging her arms, swaying and bending her long, thin body. She kept her arms flying as she swayed toward Annie.

"We...new age, free spirits, freeeeee spirits," she murmured dramatically. She said a few other things too, but Annie didn't understand. Then in a flash she took Annie's notebook from her and slid it along the polished floor toward the wall. Before she realized it, Annie was being pulled gently onto the floor and encouraged to move and sway, too. "Goooooo with the music..." the teacher murmured.

The music was barely loud enough for Annie to hear, and it was somewhat distorted. But she could feel the rhythm and the vibrations on the wooden floor. She sensed that only a few girls were still watching her now. Most of them seemed wrapped up in being free spirits. Annie was surprised to find herself moving a little. She shuffled her feet once or twice and turned her hips. It was an odd feeling. Was she dancing?

"That's right, girls," the teacher shouted. "That's... gooooooooo with it..... Loooooooose yourselves.... spirit flow...deep...other selves...."

Soon Annie found herself in front of a long mirror. She paused. There she caught a glimpse of a strange new girl. Her hair seemed to shine as it bounced. The half-moon on the chain around her neck slid back and forth on her skin. For a minute, she forgot that she was nervous and frightened. She actually sensed a light and freeeeee feeling.

Then the music ended and everyone came to a stop. The teacher called a break and started taking class roll.

Annie looked around the gym at all the bodies puffing and panting. Bets was there, too. She tried to catch Annie's eye, but Annie pretended that she had to rearrange her leg warmers.

Next to Annie, a Hispanic girl smiled shyly. Annie surprised herself by smiling back.

After class Annie noticed that this girl had the P.E. locker across from hers. While they were changing their clothes, Bets appeared.

"...catch both at the same time," Bets said cheerfully. "Do you know...Annie? This...Carlotta... Mexico City...ago. Carlotta, Annie...started today."

Again, the two girls exchanged smiles.

"So...sign up for the dance...soon.... Think about...and help...." Bets said and dashed off.

"She's in charge of everything.... maybe...president of the United States someday...." Carlotta laughed.

Annie laughed, too. She wanted to say something, but she didn't know what.

Carlotta said something about not being able to dance. Annie wondered if she had gotten it completely wrong. That didn't make sense.

"You can't dance?" she finally asked. From Carlotta's face and response, Annie figured that her voice didn't sound too nasal and strange and that she understood Annie. Hearing people couldn't always understand the deaf who were able to speak. Annie felt relieved.

"My family...very religious...." Carlotta shrugged. As she explained more, she bent to tie her shoes, and Annie missed the rest. *Maybe Carlotta's family was against dancing or music because their church didn't allow it*, Annie decided. Whatever the reason, it seemed curious. And it meant that Carlotta, also, was somewhat out of place at Eldorado.

Annie went to her next class. Biology. Mr. Tillis was busy at the back of the room. But there was a seating chart at the front. A. Meredith was assigned to a front table. It was a good thing, too. She needed to be at the front. Especially in a noisy room and with a teacher who had a mustache.

Two boys were already seated at the high table—Taylor somebody or other, who sneered at her, and a boy named Brad Snapdragon, who was wearing a pair of ski sunglasses. They were the kind you could see through from the inside, but had mirrors on the outside. They gave Annie the creeps.

As the class was starting, a girl rushed in and headed toward Annie's table. Annie recognized her at once. She was the girl from the tennis team whom Annie had seen in the hall the day before. Her name was Rita. She gave a lively greeting to the two boys. Then, she slid onto her stool and crossed her legs, just the way a model would.

Brad jumped down from his stool, went over to Rita, and put his arm around her waist. Rita pretended that she didn't like it and wriggled away, but not very far.

Rita whispered something to him. Then she asked Brad a question about his mother. Annie caught the word *TV*. *Not many people in the world have Brad's last name. I wonder if Judy Snapdragon, of "The Judy Snapdragon Show," is his mother?* Annie thought.

Mr. Tillis called the class to order. The students opened their books, and Mr. Tillis started speaking. Annie didn't catch any of it. He went to the blackboard and wrote in a scrawled handwriting, taking up a great deal of space. For two or three minutes he talked and wrote. All the time his back was toward Annie. It was impossible to understand anything.

At Sandhurst, the teachers encouraged the students to look to each other for help. They didn't want anyone sitting blankly when it was possible to turn to another person. Casually, Annie leaned over and looked at Rita's notes to get an idea about what was going on.

But Rita slapped her hand on top of her paper and glared at Annie with a look that said, *What's wrong with you? Can't you do your own work?* Rita whispered to Brad, rolled her eyes toward Annie, and made an awful face.

Then, before Annie realized it, something else was happening. Mr. Tillis seemed to be talking directly to her.

"...forgot about you.... been getting information? ...hard to remember...problem...."

Annie clutched the edge of the table.

Before she had a chance to catch her breath, Mr. Tillis turned to Rita. He seemed to be telling Rita to act as a class assistant to Annie. Annie thought he was saying that Rita should cooperate...help her out.

Then Mr. Tillis simply returned to the blackboard and wrote: Biology —the study of living things. A certain form, size, life span.

1. Begins
2. Grows
3. Matures
4. Dies

Annie's eyes turned from the blackboard back to Rita. It was clear that Rita wanted nothing to do with Annie, and now she had been told to be her class aide. Rita snapped her tongue against the roof of her mouth in disgust, and Brad and Taylor poked their fingers in their ears and made mocking sounds and faces.

Annie might be able to tell Ms. Gordon that she was having a problem in biology. But how could she say that kids were making fun of her? Tattling was something that nursery school children did. Besides, if she said anything and it got back to them, who knew what else they might do?

CHAPTER FIVE

Annie stood at the cafeteria doorway. Her notebook and lunch bag were pressed tightly to her chest. The noise of the voices and the high-pitched clanging of the dishes and silverware rang uncomfortably in her ears.

Where could she sit? Her eyes scanned the vast room. Then she remembered the patio. She began to move toward it, edging along the wall. Outside she found several picnic tables filled with people. A few students sat on the lawn.

Clutching her notebook and lunch bag tighter, she headed for the grass.

"...nnie!"

Annie turned and found Carlotta behind her.

"Didn't you hear me?...called your name over and over," Carlotta said. She was squinting in the bright sunlight.

"Oh." Annie said.

"...you looked lost.... thought you...sit...friends over...." Carlotta turned and pointed to a tree.

"Thanks," Annie said. She wished she had said more than a word. Carlotta seemed sweet and friendly, and there was nothing threatening about her. So far, Carlotta didn't know that Annie was deaf, but Annie wondered how Carlotta would react when she found out.

Carlotta introduced Annie to Herma and Tracy. At least she thought those were the girls' names. They talked and ate at the same time, so it was hard to pick up much of the conversation. All Annie could figure out was that they were talking about driver's ed, and Carlotta appeared both disappointed and angry. Annie was curious to find out what Carlotta was talking about. Finally she worked up the courage to ask.

"I'm not allowed to take driver's ed...." Carlotta answered. "...father won't sign...slip. So stubborn! ...afraid of everything new...things I try.... I get so mad."

Annie was trying to think of something comforting to say when Herma asked Annie if she had Tillis for driver's ed. Annie nodded, keeping to herself her thoughts that it was a waste of time for her. All Mr. Tillis had done was pull the shades down, turn on a road safety movie, and leave the room. It had a fuzzy narration, and the whole movie went over Annie's head.

It's only a matter of time, though, Annie reminded herself. As soon as she failed both that class and biology, there would be another meeting about her. Maybe behind her back. Maybe with her. Who knew exactly how it would happen? Either way, the end result would be the same. Eldorado would have to admit that they couldn't keep her any longer.

The girls started talking about something else, and another question was asked of Annie. It took a while before Annie caught on that she was being spoken to. Carlotta had noticed that Annie wasn't joining in and asked if Annie didn't hear, or if they were getting too personal by asking too many questions.

Annie pressed her fingers into the apple she was holding. She didn't know what to answer. Should she say something or not? Her pulse raced. Suddenly she blurted out, "I have kind of a problem," but she stopped herself before she went on. What had she done? She was shocked at herself.

"Are you sick or something?" Carlotta asked.

Annie shook her head. "Excuse me, but I have to go." she said, getting up and hurrying across the lawn and out the back gate of the schoolyard. She hadn't even taken her lunch and notebook. She didn't know exactly what had made her leave now instead of running out of homeroom when she had been so embarrassed. Maybe it was because she was starting to like Carlotta, and Annie was afraid that once Carlotta found out she was deaf, she might not want Annie as a friend.

At the apartment building, Annie pushed her key into the front door. After pausing momentarily to look at this strange place she was supposed to call home, she ran to her room and flung herself across her bed. The Hug-Me bear sitting on her pillow reminded her of all she missed in her other world. The bear only made her feel worse.

She didn't know how long she lay there sobbing, but it seemed a very long time. Finally, worn-out, she sat up and wiped her face. It was not quite two o'clock. She wondered if Kay were in Mr. Silver's class right now and what they were doing. Annie got out her stationery and wrote a letter to Kay, pleading with her to come visit soon.

After sealing the envelope, she went to the corner mailbox and dropped it in the slot. When she returned home, she wandered aimlessly from room to room until she settled in front of the TV and flicked around the channels, using the remote control, until she found a game show. Sitting in the bentwood rocker where her mother used to rock her, Annie watched the contestants fret and worry, jump up and down with excitement when they won, and look defeated when they lost. One woman threw her arms around the host to kiss him and wouldn't let go. People on game shows had faces that really came alive. Commercials were good to watch, too, because they were easy to understand.

Annie was watching a shampoo commercial when Gil walked in. He was beaming about something. It unnerved Annie that he was so happy only a short time after their move.

He dropped a package on a table and signed to Annie that he had registered for classes at a community college. He told her that he had gotten a part-time job with the campus food services, too.

"And I was standing in line when I met this girl," he went on. "And we got to talking, and before I knew it we ended up going out for ice cream. Her name's Joanne. She's really terrific."

Annie didn't answer. She just rocked faster and faster.

Gil was still signing excitedly when he began to realize that something was not quite right.

"What are you doing home at this hour, anyway?" he asked, puzzled.

Annie glared, telling him with her eyes that it was none of his business.

Gil flicked off the TV. "What's going on?" he asked.

"You can see, can't you?" Annie answered, signing

hastily. "I'm not at school. I'm here. I'm here because I want to be."

"Oh, wow!" Gil smacked his hand on his forehead, indicating that he was about to give up.

"I hate it, Gil," Annie told him. "I really do. I never want to go back."

"Oh, Annie..." Gil shook his head. "You've been crying. Maybe I shouldn't have pushed you to go alone. Maybe I should have come with you. What about that resource teacher? Didn't she help? Dad and I thought she seemed.... I wish things could be better. You give it a chance...."

Annie got up and stood by the window, absently staring out. She didn't want to hear any more of Gil's *maybes* and *wishes*. They were all meaningless.

"I'm sorry, Annie," Gil said, turning her toward him. "Do you want me to take you back to school now? I'll stay with you this time, if it helps."

Annie started to answer that his amends were too late, but she saw her father drive up in one of the auto shop trucks. He was wearing a green jumpsuit that all the mechanics wore, and he lumbered up the walk with his hands deep in his pockets. She ran to greet him and accompanied him into the apartment.

He didn't notice her puffy eyes, but he noticed the time and asked what she was doing home so early.

"She says she hates it, and she left in the middle of the day," Gil answered for her. "She hasn't given herself a chance. I just know if she gives it a little more time, she can...."

Annie stomped her feet, not caring if they called her a child and not caring if the people in the apartment below heard her. She didn't know what to do with her anger any more. A minute ago Gil had tried apologizing and had offered to make it up to her.

Now, with her father home, he and her father were teaming up against her again.

"I don't belong there," Annie cried.

Annie's father wiped his arm across his forehead and then rubbed his hands on his cheeks, hard.

"Gil's right. You're making a snap judgment," he told her. "...and after all we did to convince them that you do belong there."

"You didn't convince *me!*" Annie said. Afterward, she ran to her father and put her arms around his neck. "Oh, please, Dad. Please let me go back to Sandhurst. I'll do anything. Can't we figure out a way?"

Slowly, her father put his arms around her and held her for a minute. Then he pulled away and rubbed his cheeks again.

"I don't see how," he said, signing awkwardly, and then giving up. "Don't you think that we tried to think of every possibility from the start?"

"You don't know what it's like," she murmured. "Neither of you do."

"We're doing the best we can," her father said. "Can you give it a little more time, Annie? Can you do that?"

Annie sighed. It wasn't exactly a *yes*, but it wasn't exactly a *no* either. It was a kind of defeat, but there was still hope that she could go back to Sandhurst.

Gil playfully turned up the ends of Annie's mouth to force a smile.

"Come on, why don't you put on your sweats and I'll take you to the gym with me," he offered.

"Thanks. But no thanks," Annie answered. "That's your thing. I guess I'll just get supper started early."

CHAPTER SIX

"Annie Meredith, ...for you," the P.E. aide told her toward the end of class.

"What?" Annie asked.

"...message for you...go to room fourteen."

"Room fourteen?" Annie asked to be certain. "What for?"

"I don't know," the aide answered. "This note...delivered." She held up a pink slip.

Annie stood and walked toward the locker room. She was aware that several people were watching her. But people watched when anyone was called out of class. They watched when someone was called on and when someone came in late.

As she headed down the stairs, she wondered whom she was going to see. It wasn't a call to pick up her notebook, which she had left on the lawn in the middle of lunch. Carlotta had retrieved that and brought it to her in her homeroom when she returned to school the next day. Fourteen was not the resource room. Was it the principal's office?

Maybe the longed for moment was here. Maybe the principal was going to seriously question her ability to stay at Eldorado. She stopped on the stair landing. Until now that was exactly what she had been waiting for. Now she wasn't so sure she actually wanted to be kicked out of school. How would that feel?

Room fourteen did not turn out to be the principal's office. It was the student newspaper office. Sitting at a typewriter, with long legs sprawled out in front of him, was a boy Annie had seen before. He was the tennis player who had been walking with Rita the day she went to meet Ms. Gordon. The school was beginning to seem smaller.

The boy was pecking at the typewriter keys. Annie hesitated to go inside. She lingered at the doorway a minute before he looked up and noticed her standing there.

"Hi," he said with the flashy smile Annie remembered seeing that day in the hall. "Are you Annie Meredith?"

Annie nodded.

"I'm Michael Hale. Reporter for the *Eldorado Post*.... story on new students...like to talk to you...."

Sometimes his voice dropped or he brushed his hand over his mouth. But Annie understood that he wanted to interview her for a newspaper article or story. Only, of course, he didn't know that she was deaf. What would he write about her, anyway? He seemed to be asking if she had time to talk.

No, no, not now or ever! she thought. Too much was happening too fast.

Michael had several names in front of him. Hers was in the middle. She didn't know why it was included. She was a special student whose name didn't belong on that list.

He reached for a pen and a spiral notebook.

"I...I..." Annie began. "I don't think I..."

"Oh, don't worry, Annie," Michael interrupted,

41

looking genuinely sympathetic. "I won't embarrass you with personal questions. Really, I...few minutes of your time."

Annie kept shaking her head *no*.

"I don't want to upset you...."

Annie was ready to turn and run again. But she didn't. She didn't want to keep running. Did she really want to be a high school student like everyone else? Maybe she did.

"I'll try," she found herself saying shakily.

"Great...sit down," he said, perching himself on a table and starting to scribble. "You're a...more right?"

"What?"

"A...more"

Annie still didn't know what he was saying. Her eyes glazed over, and she blinked. She hated to ask again, but she did.

"I'm sorry, what did you say?"

"Sophomore...tenth grade?"

It was humiliating to admit, but Annie nodded.

"...go last year?"

"Just some other school," she answered, skipping over it lightly, hoping that he would go on to something else. "Not a very interesting place..."

Michael put down his pen and notebook. "You...feeling really uptight.... can see that. Take it easy. Maybe forget this for now...talk another time, okay?"

Annie felt deeply relieved. She had tried. She hadn't run out. And she was proud of herself for that much.

Michael Hale smiled. Annie had never seen a boy smile so kindly and with so much understanding. *He could teach Gil a thing or two*, she thought.

By the time Annie left the newspaper office,

second period had started. In biology she found Mr. Tillis at the blackboard writing about cells—how every living thing was made up of cells, and how Robert Hook had discovered the first cells when he studied a piece of cork under a microscope.

Annie sat down. Neither Rita, Brad, nor Taylor were at the table. Were all three absent? Could this be her lucky day? But it wasn't. A minute later, they came in together laughing and acting as if they were at a party. They walked in front of the teacher, and Annie didn't see even one of them say "excuse me."

But Mr. Tillis didn't ignore them as he had done before. He began to shout and scold. With the rise in his voice, Annie was able to catch a few words.

"...rude...enough...call in...parents...." Annie had never seen Mr. Tillis's face come so alive.

Rita sat with her crossed-over leg swinging back and forth. Every so often, she flicked her blond hair away from her face with a quick sweeping motion. Every time she did, Taylor made some kind of muffled, wild-animal sound.

Mr. Tillis turned his attention to a microscope. When he did, Rita suddenly turned to Annie and asked, "Why...you stare at me like...?"

Annie was taken aback. She tried not to look at Rita. Annie then caught Brad saying something to Rita about Annie taking up classroom space. "...so dumb...."

"...me stuck sitting next to...bug-eyes...." Rita said.

Annie felt her neck burning. Her hands clutched her open book. Mr. Tillis looked up from the microscope and asked a question. Everyone took out papers and handed them forward. They were already written on both sides.

Before she knew it, Mr. Tillis was standing over Annie asking for her paper.

What paper? She had not heard anything about a paper.

"...yesterday...told class...paper...."

Annie had not caught a word about it. She thought he had announced a test on Monday.

"I...I..." she stammered.

"...not have?"

Annie shook her head.

"If you want to stay...better...work at it like everyone.... no time for special...for anyone."

Annie bit the side of her mouth. Then she tried to speak. She started to explain that it wasn't her fault.

Mr. Tillis sighed and turned to Rita. It was hard to catch his words even though he was standing near her, but she understood in general that he was asking Rita what happened. Hadn't he told Rita to help the new deaf girl?

Annie hid her face in her hands. How could this be happening? A minute later Mr. Tillis dismissed the class, and Rita tossed a note at her. It read:

I have to get to my next class early.
TOO BAD!

Annie's mouth went dry, and she hurried out to the water fountain in the hall. By the time she returned to the room for driver's ed, Mr. Tillis had set up the movie projector. When the film was ready, he pulled the shades and snapped down the movie screen from the wall over the front blackboard.

The minute everyone was seated, he turned off the lights and switched on the projector. Annie heard background music swell and the drone of a low voice. The title came on the screen, "Right-of-Way Rules."

Old cars from the sixties drove back and forth across street intersections. *Stopping, starting, right lane, signal, slow, safe...*None of it made any sense to Annie. Anyway, all she could think about was the incident in biology and the gnawing ache she felt. She was beginning to really hate that class.

She liked her next class, art, best. At first she liked it because everyone worked independently. But she was surprised at how she had become caught up in drawing. At the end of the session, when one of the other students tapped her to let her know that class was over, she was startled to realize how fast the time had gone.

During resource, Ms. Gordon offered Annie a mint. She kept a dish of them on her desk. It was one of the ways Ms. Gordon showed friendship and attempted to make her students feel comfortable.

Annie hesitated at first.

"Go on," Ms. Gordon urged.

Annie shrugged. Ms. Gordon seemed so intent on being the friendly, helpful teacher. Annie didn't want to hurt her feelings by refusing. So she reached for a mint, popped it into her mouth, and let it melt slowly. Then she opened her art folder. She was glad she had something nice to show Ms. Gordon. It would be a good distraction, since she had made up her mind not to tattle on the kids in biology.

Annie handed Ms. Gordon a still-life sketch. The art teacher had arranged a hodge-podge of objects on a table—a copper kettle, a cut melon with seeds, a long-handled wooden spoon, a straw doll, a Mexican hat, and a serape that draped over the side of the table. Annie had done three sketches. She showed Ms. Gordon the one she liked best.

In return she received a nice compliment. *It was a good sketch*, Annie thought, beaming with pride.

Signing, Ms. Gordon asked, "How do you like your classes in general?"

"They're okay," Annie finally answered simply. She didn't want to sound too enthusiastic. She wasn't going to tattle, but she didn't want to give the impression that things were going well for her, either.

Next, they settled down to working on vocabulary and pronunciation. Some of the words were from her biology lessons, and others were new idea and concept words listed by Ms. Gordon.

That was followed by a writing lesson. Writing lessons at Sandhurst had not interested Annie much. She had usually waited until the last minute with such assignments, or avoided them altogether when she could get away with it.

Ms. Gordon explained how to set down the main idea and then back it up with subpoints. She called the main idea sentence the *power* or *topic sentence*. They worked on an example together. *This lesson isn't too bad*, Annie thought. *At least it makes sense*.

After that, Ms. Gordon handed Annie a paperback book to read for pleasure. No book report. No questions to answer or blanks to fill in. Just reading for fun. That sounded okay to Annie. It was a collection of short stories called *Dear Bill, Remember Me?* That was the title of one of the stories. Two other story titles looked especially interesting, "Chocolate Pudding," and "Mimi, the Fish."

There were a few minutes of resource left so Annie started reading "Mimi." It was about a girl who didn't want to invite friends over to her home behind the butcher shop, and her mother couldn't understand why. Carlotta had found out from Bets that Annie was deaf, and Carlotta had answered, *so what?* Annie and Carlotta had talked during P.E. and lunch, and Annie thought she would share this story with her.

At the end of resource, Annie put a bookmark in the book to mark her place and reached for one more mint before leaving. As she did, Ms. Gordon asked again how things were going. Was there anything Annie wanted to discuss?

Remembering what had happened in biology, Annie felt a wave of nausea. But she only lowered her eyes and murmured, "No. Everything's fine."

CHAPTER SEVEN

"Kay!"

"Annie!"

"You look great!"

"So do you!"

"Come in," Annie cried, signing excitedly. "I thought that bus would never arrive."

Annie's father leaned against the door frame. He had picked up Kay at the bus station during his lunch hour, and now he had to hurry back to the auto shop. Annie was grateful for the favor. She and Kay both thanked him.

"Glad...see a smile on your face," he said. "...don't know what time I'll be home for supper. But I'll see you girls later.... nice afternoon together."

"We will," Annie said happily.

After her father left, she squealed as she signed to Kay, "You look great!"

"You said that already," Kay laughed.

"That's a new lipstick shade you're wearing," Annie said, noticing Kay's lips.

"Rose Festival," Kay told her, fingerspelling the name. "It's high-gloss."

"Really? I just bought a new high-gloss, too."

Annie picked up Kay's weekend bag and brought it into her bedroom.

"So this is your new place," Kay signed. "It's not as bad as you described in your letters. It looks cozy. Like our house."

"I'm starting to get used to it," Annie answered. "But sometimes when I wake up, I still forget where I am. I've bumped into the wall a few times when I've been half asleep."

Kay kicked her shoes off and sat down cross-legged on Annie's bed.

Annie settled herself on the furry oval rug, hugging her knees.

"Tell me everything about your school," Kay urged.

Annie sighed, hugged her knees tighter for a second, then let go so she could go on signing. A lot had happened during her first two weeks in school. She had a great deal to tell.

"It's awful," she began, "You can't imagine how awful."

At once she went on to tell Kay about the classes and the teachers, and how out-of-place she felt. She talked about Carlotta and Elizabeth, "Bets," and the disaster with Michael Hale in the newspaper office.

"What about those kids at your biology table?" Kay asked. "Are they any better?"

"Worse," Annie answered, and she explained the latest incident.

Kay lowered her eyes momentarily. She truly understood how Annie felt. It was so good to have Kay to talk to. Annie wished the weekend would last forever.

Until today they had never had to explain anything to each other. But now, Annie was stepping into a new world, and it was strange having to explain it to her best friend.

Kay was eager to hear everything, and she urged Annie to tell more. She wanted to know every detail.

Finally Kay asked, "How long do you think you'll have to stay at Eldorado?"

Annie remembered her tearful promise to Kay that she would not make it and that she would be back with her in a short time. But now she didn't really know what would happen to her, and she didn't know what to answer. She shrugged and hoped that Kay would not press her further. Some parts of her school day, and some of the kids, she realized, she enjoyed.

Quickly, she changed the subject and asked Kay to tell her what was happening at Sandhurst. "You can't imagine how much I miss you and everyone there," Annie moaned, grabbing her Hug-Me bear and cradling it in her lap.

"Yes, I can imagine," Kay sympathized. "Believe me, I can. Can you imagine how much I miss *you?*"

"I get a huge lump in my throat just thinking about it," Annie made the sign for *thinking*, but she used both hands to show she really meant it.

"I hardly know where to begin," Kay signed slowly, while she considered the matter. "Well, first, everyone sends regards. Mr. Silver, Miss Ross, Mr. Watts, Jill, Stephanie, Paul, Cheryl, and just everyone...even the custodian, Ernie..."

Annie pictured each person as Kay signed the names.

"Mr. Silver's message was actually this," Kay added, and she made a thumbs-up sign.

Annie smiled.

"And guess what else?" Kay said. "Ever since you left, Jody Pratt follows me around all day."

"Oh, no..."

"You wouldn't believe what she did to her hair..."

"She dyed it?"

"How did you know? It came out red-orange. Fiery red-orange. It's absolutely blinding."

Annie and Kay burst into laughter.

Kay continued with more school stories and gossip, and when they started to wind down, Annie suggested they go into the kitchen and bake something fattening and sinful. They had often baked together at Kay's house.

Annie pulled a cookbook out of the last unpacked carton and started leafing through it.

"How's this? Almond Date Roll?"

Kay wrinkled up her nose in refusal.

"How about Raspberry Nut Cream?" Annie suggested next, "I think we have all the stuff."

Kay licked her lips in response while Annie handed her some butter, sugar, and a box of wafers. "Here, you can melt the butter and crush the wafers. Then, mix it with a fourth cup of sugar to make the crust," she said.

Annie took the job of mixing the cream cheese with part of the butter and two cups of powdered sugar to spread over the crust. Then they boiled water for the raspberry jello. As soon as the jello was dissolved and somewhat thickened by using ice cubes, Kay started to pour it into the crust.

"No! Wait!" Annie stopped her, grabbing for the canister. "The nuts have to go in first."

To top it off, Annie whipped the whipping cream and spread it over the jello, while Kay sprinkled the last of the nuts over that.

Annie stood back and looked at it. "Yechhh. Disgusting," she signed.

"It's not so bad," Kay signed. "Maybe after it's been in the fridge for a while, it'll look better."

"I don't think so...but it *is* fattening and sinful," Annie laughed.

Annie and Kay turned around at the same time. Gil had entered the kitchen.

"Hey, look who's here!" he said, tickling Kay under the chin.

"Gil," Annie poked him, reminding him that she had told him not to do that to Kay. Kay didn't like being treated like a child any more than Annie did. Besides, Kay had already turned seventeen. Some of Gil's girlfriends were that age, and he certainly never tickled *them* under the chin.

"Sorry," Gil, signing, apologized to Kay. "I'm so used to it. I still think of you as my little sister's friend."

"You better learn to get *un*-used to it," Annie advised.

Annie and Kay sat down at the kitchen table. Surprisingly, Gil joined them.

"So, what's going on around here?" he asked.

"Nothing," Annie answered. She waited for him to get up and leave. But he didn't. He took a banana from the fruit bowl in the center of the table and started peeling it. *Did Gil want to hang around with them?* Annie wondered. He had never done that before.

"Don't you have something to do?" she suggested. "Kay and I have a lot to talk about."

"Go ahead and talk," Gil said, trying to sign with the banana still in his hand. "I won't bother you."

"It's private."

"Honest. I won't bother you. Go ahead."

"We could go back to your room," Kay suggested to Annie.

Gil stuffed a quarter of the banana into his mouth. While he chewed, he signed, "I have a better idea. I'll take you both out for a drive."

"What happened?" Annie asked him. "Did Joanne break a date with you?"

Gil didn't answer. "Oh, come on," he urged. "We can show Kay around San Lucas."

"I don't know," Annie protested, turning to Kay to get her reaction.

"Whatever you want," Kay shrugged.

"No, I don't feel like it," Annie told Gil.

"Come on," Gil persisted. "How can you stand sitting around inside all the time?"

"I like it," Annie lied.

"Hah!" he snorted, disbelieving.

"Well...do you want to, Kay?" Annie hesitated.

"If you do."

Annie gave in, and within minutes they were ready to leave.

Gil drove around the immediate neighborhood for a few minutes, pointing out the library and police station, a bronze statue honoring local war veterans, and a small mall. After that, he said it would be nice to take Kay out to the bird sanctuary, and on the way they could drive by the park and Eldorado High.

As Gil cruised past the park he exclaimed at the sight of a girl on the tennis court. "Wow!" ...move! ...power in those legs! And...gorgeous, too!"

Annie glanced out of the car window. The girl whom Gil was talking about was none other than Rita Leland. And the person she was playing with was Michael Hale. Annie crouched down in the seat so they wouldn't see her. It was all Gil's fault! Annie had been just fine at home with Kay. But Gil had to come along and insist they go out for a ride. A perfectly happy afternoon ruined!

CHAPTER EIGHT

Annie felt a tap on her shoulder in homeroom. There was a note for her. It was from Bets. *That girl just never gives up*, Annie thought. She opened the note and read:

Hi — a week from Friday the politics club is meeting during lunch period in 114 — we're having a "LIVE" guest speaker! State Senator Earl Gleason. Wait until you see him. He's absolutely fabulous! Please, please come!!!
P.S.
Where'd you get that sweater? I've been looking all over for one like it — only I want it in a solid color. — Bets "

Annie smiled to herself. How could she continue to ignore Bets? Bets made it impossible.

Annie ripped a piece of paper from her notebook and wrote back:

Hi! I got this sweater a long time ago — and I didn't get it here.

After she signed her name, she started thinking about the other part of Bets's note. Maybe she would go to that meeting and try to hear that state senator speak. She might be able to bring up a new subject with her father and Gil at the dinner table. If she discussed something important like the government, wouldn't they be impressed! They might even start treating her more like an adult. She added a P.S. saying that maybe she'd come to the politics club meeting.

When she looked up, she saw that the homeroom teacher was reading from the announcement sheet.

"Hall monitors...too many students in the halls after classes have started. Starting today late slips will be given out to offenders...detention...Debate club meeting changed to...locker inspection... week...won't know...board of education...Pep rally Friday afternoon...

"One more thing...school equipment...disappearing....typewriters missing and...smaller items from the office....warning. Anyone caught...dealt with...anyone with information, please tell a staff member. You will not be held...or responsible...kept confidential...

"Okay, any questions?"

There were never any questions after these announcements. Most students barely listened to them in the first place.

Annie folded her note, addressed it to Bets, and passed it along to her. When the bell rang, Bets waited for her at the door, and they walked out together. Bets told Annie that Annie would probably fall in love with Senator Gleason at first sight. She added that if Annie happened to find the sweater in a nearby store, would she please let her know.

Later, in driver's ed, the window shades were not

drawn, and the projector was not out. Mr. Tillis was standing at the front of the room, impatiently tapping his foot.

"Okay, now...finish this quiz and..." he said when the last student was seated.

Annie panicked. She had heard him announce a quiz, but she thought he had said Wednesday, not Tuesday. She hadn't studied her booklet. And she hadn't found anyone in class yet to ask about borrowing movie notes.

It was too late now. Annie glanced at the question sheet passed to her.

"At all intersections with stop or yield signs, slow down and be prepared to stop. Yield to cars already _____ (fill in the blank). Signal _____ and yield to approaching traffic until it's safe to make a complete turn."

That was hard, so she skipped it and went on.

"When you hear the siren of a police car, fire engine, ambulance or other emergency vehicle, you must _____." *Pull over immediately.* That answer she knew, but it was only one of two on the whole sheet that she did know. Two out of sixteen questions. She was left with a terrible pit-in-the-stomach feeling. If Gil or her father found out that she had failed something as easy as a driver's ed quiz, they would never stop teasing her.

It wasn't her fault, though. She was trying. She really was. *Maybe I'll mention this problem to Ms. Gordon today,* she thought. *And I can take a makeup quiz.*

When it was time for resource, Annie hurried downstairs. But she stopped just outside the glass door leading to Ms. Gordon's office. Someone was already in there. An adult, holding a key chain. Annie guessed it was a mother. On closer look, Annie saw that she was red-faced and angry. Annie couldn't catch everything the woman was saying, but she caught enough of the woman's lip movements to understand.

She was saying "...with problems...deaf and blind...taking time away from...normal students...not learning...Rita doesn't have to give...time with...deaf as a brick...busy...study and tennis...why should she..."

So that was it! This was Rita Leland's mother. She thought Annie had no right to be at Eldorado. She didn't want Annie to take up Rita's important time. How many other people didn't like Annie besides Rita, Rita's mother, and Mr. Tillis? But why should anyone hate her and make accusations against her? She hadn't done anything. She had just as much right as anyone to be here in school. There were even lots of students here who didn't care about getting an education at all.

The muscles in her neck grew taut, and her head pounded. Before this, she had mostly been brooding and feeling lonely and sorry for herself. Now, she felt a strong wave of anger.

Annie watched as Ms. Gordon tried to calm Mrs. Leland, but it was no use. Mrs. Leland spoke her piece and stormed out, passing Annie without even realizing that *she* was the horrible girl who was deaf as a brick!

Ms. Gordon caught sight of Annie. She clapped her hands over her mouth, realizing at once that Annie had understood the scene. With a face that showed deep concern and regret, she ushered Annie into her office and tried to explain.

"I'm so sorry," she apologized. "There are some people like that...they won't listen. They won't even try to understand."

Annie sat down, shakily fingering her necklace. Many times, her mother had tried to tell her the world was made up of all kinds of people. And that included some who were insensitive and cruel. But everyone has to deal with them sometime, she explained, not just people like Annie who have harder barriers to cross than most. If her mother expected Annie to meet people like Mrs. Leland, why would she want Annie to go out into this other world?

"But that woman has no right..." Annie insisted to Ms. Gordon. "And neither does Rita..."

Ms. Gordon asked Annie to tell her what had been going on. Annie didn't spill out everything the way she had to Kay, but she told the resource teacher a great deal. Signing dramatically, she explained about Mr. Tillis and his biology and driver's ed classes, except she hesitated to mention the three kids at her biology table. Who knows what they would do if they found out she had snitched?

"What about Rita Leland?" Ms. Gordon asked.

Annie shrugged. "Well, she just doesn't have time to help me...it's okay..." she lied.

"I hate to see you so upset," Ms. Gordon said and signed.

"It's okay," Annie repeated. "Please don't say anything to them or to Mr. Tillis. It would be embarrassing for me."

"We only want to do what's best for you," Ms. Gordon said.

"I know," Annie answered. It was odd, but even though she would rather be at Sandhurst instead of Eldorado, she still had the right to be any place she chose.

At home, Annie found her father asleep on the sofa. He was stretched out on his back, still wearing his grimy jumpsuit. Annie realized that he must be extremely tired.

She put her books down and tiptoed past him, but he stirred and opened his eyes.

"Oh...home already? I only meant to take a ten-minute snooze." He pushed himself up on one elbow and rubbed his eyes.

"What a dream I was having," he said. "At first it was your mother in the dream, ...then...turned into another woman....hazy, but I...happy to have someone there with me again. She fixed my tie, and she had on this nice perfume.... same perfume that I gave your mother for her birthday."

Annie remembered her mother's delight in the perfume.

She sat across from her father on the rocker and looked at him. His face was leathered, and his expression weary. Lately, he hardly bothered to shave in the morning.

Something that had not occurred to her came to her mind now, and she was a little ashamed that she had not considered it earlier. Her father was lonely without a wife. It had been a long time. He needed someone.

Annie went over to the sofa and sat on the edge near him.

"I'm sorry the way things turned out," he told her slowly and directly. "I never wanted to move. The last thing in the world I wanted was to take you away from Sandhurst and your friends."

"I know," Annie answered. Since they'd moved, she had felt a growing distance at home. Now she was beginning to understand that her father didn't mean to be distant. The Meredith family had had its share of problems, and her father had slipped into a shell, too, the way she often did.

"I wish...possible...make things better for you," her father told her.

"I know that, too," she answered.

Her father rubbed his eyes and stretched.

"Yup, that sure was some dream," he said.

She looked at him sympathetically. They all missed her mother terribly.

Annie's father took hold of her arm. "How about if I take you out to dinner tonight?" he asked. "Can you...the mood for barbecued ribs?"

"Absolutely," Annie answered. "But Gil won't be home until late."

"I mean just the two of us," he said, pointing to her and then to himself. "It would be a good time for you and me to catch up on things."

Annie gave her father a thumbs-up sign and then a hug.

CHAPTER NINE

Annie stared at the pile of clothes in need of ironing. She had already put the job off for days. What was one more day? She felt the urge to go outside to the park instead.

She thought she might find a comfortable spot and sit down and write a long letter to Kay. After gathering her stationery, a pen, and a fashion magazine, she set out, walking briskly and with a bounce in her step almost as lively as Gil's. She was feeling freeeee... letting her spirit gooooo.

It was a nice autumn day, clear and crisp. The park was full of activity. Two young boys whizzed past her on skateboards. She hadn't been aware of them coming from behind her, and she was startled when they suddenly appeared.

After she caught her breath, she wandered over to the recreation building and browsed in front of the bulletin board. It was full of notices.

Fall Teen Volunteer Program
Be a Buddy to Younger Kids!
Crafts, sports, games, nature walks, etc.

**Have you got any arts and crafts materials
hanging around your house???
Don't throw them out. We'll take them off
your hands.
Ask Corky Cutler, rec director**

**Picnic plans for thanking summer volunteers
to be announced**

**Baby Sitting—Super Team
Lynn Blue and Debby Nelson
Call 555-1067**

**Lost and Found—Summer Clearance
skateboard
2 lunchboxes—one with thermos
tennis racket press
lefthanded mitt
assorted jackets, sweatshirts, etc.
painted rock
about 20 sneakers—some matching**

The notices reminded Annie of Bets's Rock-a-thon poster. Bets was still begging Annie to participate. Annie wasn't ready to go to a dance—she wouldn't be comfortable. But she had agreed to help Bets get the gym ready.

Annie wandered up a jogging path toward the basketball and tennis courts. She thought she might settle under a big tree, write her letter, and browse through her fashion magazine.

Annie was surprised to see Michael Hale. He was on a tennis court, but he wasn't playing. He was showing several young children how to swing a racket. Annie stood in the distance for a few minutes, watching. He was very patient with them, especially when one child stopped paying attention and started hitting another child.

Annie guessed that Michael was part of the volunteer program. Maybe he was a buddy. *How nice*, she thought. Another thought occurred to her, too. A puzzling one. *Why was such a kind person so friendly with someone like Rita Leland?*

All of a sudden, the two boys on skateboards, who had startled Annie earlier, whizzed by again. The smaller boy hit a wide crack in the pavement. Whap! He was in the air feet first—and then down in a flash—landing heavily on his right arm.

Annie ran to him. He lay dazed. His arm was bent under his body, and his face was twisted in pain. Then he burst into tears.

"I can't move!" he cried.

The other boy spun around and came back to see what had happened. A small crowd began to gather.

Annie could see at once that it was a serious accident. She felt sure that the arm was broken. Probably in more than one place.

"It's okay," she whispered to the boy. "You'll be fine. Let me help you."

Gently, Annie shifted him.

"...what's wrong...anyway?" the older boy asked. "...a real fake...."

It seemed that this was the younger boy's brother and he was calling the injured child a faker.

"He's not faking," Annie said knowingly. Meanwhile she looked around for something she could use to support the injured arm.

The younger boy started crying again, and Annie soothed him. She caught sight of the magazine she had dropped when she stooped down. That was it!

Perfect! Carefully, she rolled it into a tube around the boy's arm. Next, she pulled the leather belt from her jeans. Just as she was tying it around the magazine splint, Michael Hale appeared at her side. He stooped down and asked what had happened.

"His arm is badly broken," Annie answered.

"...want me to..."

Annie wasn't sure what he said, but she instructed him to call the paramedics.

As Michael started to leave Annie added, "Tell them it's a child."

As soon as Michael hurried away, she secured the improvised splint and assured the boy that help was on the way.

"It hurts real bad...terrible..."

"I know," Annie told him. "It's okay for you to cry. That's what tears are for. They're made exactly for times when people are hurt and scared. Nobody can be brave all the time, right?"

"Noooo," the boy sniffed.

"...really going...ambulance?" the brother asked, his eyes wide.

"Sure," Annie answered, then turned to the injured boy. "You'll be the most famous kid in the park. Just like being on a TV show."

Michael returned a few minutes later. Together, he and Annie got the name and address of the child so they would have it ready to give to the paramedics immediately. A short time later the paramedics arrived. As they helped the boy onto the stretcher, Annie patted his cheek and told him that maybe someday he could be a paramedic just like the men who came to his rescue. He seemed to like that and smiled at her through his tears.

After the crowd disappeared, Annie found herself

standing with Michael Hale. Only then did she start to blush. She had been too busy until that moment.

"You were terrific," Michael told her. "A...Florence Nightingale."

She smiled and shrugged. *That's a bit exaggerated,* she thought. *But he certainly has a way of making a nervous person feel comfortable.*

"Don't be...modest," he told her.

At that moment, the older boy came running back, waving Annie's belt.

"My brother is...lucky," he said. "I wish I had a broken bone."

"The way you race around on your skateboard, I'm sure you'll be next," Annie warned.

The boy's eyes lit up. "You really think so?"

Michael laughed and said something about what kids will do to get attention. Then suddenly he was asking her if she wanted to sit down on a nearby bench.

Annie truly wanted to say *yes.* Only she didn't think there was any way she could sit in the noisy outdoors and carry on a conversation. Anyway, what could she possibly talk about with him? But then he seemed sincerely interested in her. And he was a thoughtful person. There were plenty of kids at school who avoided her or even pretended they didn't see her. But Bets and Carlotta were different. Now this boy, too? Besides, wouldn't this be a surprise to Gil? And to Kay, who might not even believe it. She could hardly believe it herself.

Nervously, Annie followed Michael to the bench and sat down next to him, but not too close. She held her belt tightly in her lap and poked the belt prong in and out of one of the holes. Michael started to ask her something, and Annie realized that she couldn't pretend with him. It would only turn out to be another disaster.

There was only one thing to do—tell him straight out. She took a breath and started shakily to speak, "I don't always hear everything you say." She stopped and suddenly blurted out, "I'm deaf. I need to see your face when you talk."

"Oh. Sorry. I didn't realize," he said. "...that's why...in the school newspaper office...you...."

Annie nodded.

"Sorry," he said again.

"That's okay. You don't have to say that all the time. Sometimes it's just as hard for other people...." Annie was surprised at her ease in reassuring Michael and at how easy it had been, once she'd just *done* it, to tell Michael that she was deaf.

There was a pause, and Michael turned a tennis ball in his hand a few times. Finally he turned to Annie. "Can I ask you something?" he asked.

"Sure."

"You won't think...rude?"

"No. It's okay."

He asked her what it felt like—what it *really* felt like to be deaf. "I mean...once met a blind boy...summer camp...could figure out what...like not to see. We became friends that summer...some people never talked to him...avoided him...afraid they would say the wrong thing...no reason to leave a person standing alone...."

Michael's story went on for a few minutes. Annie could tell he was a little nervous, too. That was natural. It happened to plenty of people. Mr. Silver had talked about that from time to time. He had said that sometimes the disabled person has to help out the person he or she is just meeting by showing that new person how to be at ease.

Annie told that to Michael, and that she was glad he had asked the question so openly.

Michael breathed a sigh of relief. "That makes it easier...better...for other people.... Do you use sign language, too?"

"Oh, of course. Signing is a more natural language for the deaf. I understand a lot more with it. Anyway, speechreading and speaking aren't easy. Some people I know don't talk at all. I guess I manage okay because I wasn't born deaf. I wear two hearing aids," she added. "They help a little."

Annie's heart beat rapidly as she spoke. Was it because she had never told a hearing person so much about herself? Or was it because she liked Michael Hale? Maybe it was both.

Michael listened intently. "You speak real well, Annie. I can understand everything you say." He paused a moment and then continued, "If I turned off the TV volume...some idea of what it feels like?"

Annie shrugged and shook her head. "Not really. There's a lot more to it. You feel left out of the real world. It's hard to keep up with everything's that's happening around you."

"...hard for you in a new school?" Michael asked.

Annie nodded. She certainly didn't want to go into details about this subject after she had just talked so straightforwardly to him already. Instead, she told him about the new resource teacher and how much she was trying to help Annie.

"...don't know her...sounds nice...interesting...." he said. "Maybe I can write a newspaper story about her.... make a good feature. I'm trying...improve the newspaper this year. I...plenty of ideas."

"Is it fun working for the newspaper?" Annie asked.

"I like it okay," Michael answered. "But tennis takes up most of my outside time."

There was another pause. Annie felt self-conscious and twisted the belt between her fingers. She wondered if Michael were bored and wanted to leave but didn't know how to excuse himself politely. He didn't leave, though, so she asked him where he lived. She couldn't think of anything else to ask.

"Only a few blocks from school on the corner of Westhill and Spring. And you?"

"On the other side of the park," Annie answered.

Michael tossed the tennis ball in the air a few times and suddenly asked Annie if she wanted to go for pizza with him.

"Go for pizza with you?" Annie asked to be sure she got it right. He nodded. This was becoming more unbelievable by the minute.

"Yes!" she said, her heart fluttering wildly. Imagine! Wandering alone through the park. And now unexpectedly going to a restaurant with Michael Hale.

"Great," Michael answered. "I'm meeting the team...half hour...celebrating our win yesterday."

"Team? Tennis team?" Annie asked. "Will Rita Leland be there, too?"

"Sure. She won her match."

Annie felt a thud in her chest. No way would she go now. It had been too good to be true, anyway.

"I'm sorry," she apologized. "I can't go after all. I..."

"Why not?"

"Well...I," Annie faltered. "I...forgot. My family needs me at home, and I'm late now."

"That's too bad," Michael said. "...really a shame."

"Thanks," Annie tried to smile. She hoped that he would mention another time when they could go out for pizza together. But he didn't. He just said it was nice talking to her, and that he would see her around at school next week.

CHAPTER TEN

Annie and Bets were excused from the start of P.E. to help carry in a load of Rock-a-thon stuff from the trunk of Bets's father's car. They lugged the cartons down the halls into the gym office. When every box was accounted for, Annie brushed off her hands and started to leave. But Bets caught her and pulled her back.

"Don't you want to see what's in them?" she asked Annie.

"Maybe we shouldn't take anymore time now," Annie said. "Maybe we should change for class."

"Oh, come on..." Bets urged, already prying one carton open. "You have to see this. It's absolutely fantastic!"

Annie leaned over and took a peek. She saw a huge, round, antique mirror light.

"Isn't it great?" Bets exclaimed, her eyes lighting up. "I have to guard...with my life...it's worth a fortune!"

Annie nodded. It was fantastic. She had seen a movie about the Roaring Twenties. There had been a light just like this one hanging from the ceiling at a dance where people danced all night. The light had turned slowly, flashing reflections all around the room and onto the dancing figures.

"Oh, please come, Annie!" Bets begged, as they finally started to change into their P.E. shorts.

"No, I just can't," Annie answered. She wished Bets would stop bringing up the dance every day.

"Well, anyway," Bets said, "I'm tied with someone else for having the most pledges so far...forty-four people. I'm going to dance for...twelve hours...I think I can do it. Maybe I can lose a few pounds, too." She laughed.

In the gym, Annie and Bets found everyone doing something new today. It was *free-machine* time. Everyone was supposed to think of a machine, real or imagined, and then become it.

Some of the girls were crank-type machines with their arms flapping up and down, or around. It was easy to spot one as a word processor. Carlotta's friend, Tracy, looked like an oil pump. Some didn't resemble anything familiar.

"Pump, churn, glide, shift...that's it girls," the teacher called out, strolling up and down. "Think like your machine."

Immediately Bets became something, bending and twisting, with her tongue flashing in and out, but she started giggling and couldn't stop. The laughter was contagious. Annie stood watching. She had no idea what kind of machine to become. How silly she felt. "...no foolish...laughing...serious business...." the teacher said and turned to Annie, motioning her to "hook up and get moving."

Everyone looked silly. At least she wouldn't be alone. What finally came to her mind was an old-fashioned sewing machine that belonged to Kay's grandmother. It had left an impression on Annie because it looked so complicated.

Here goes, Annie said to herself, and she crouched

71

down, curved an arm like a wheel, and clicked her upper and lower teeth together rapidly to become the sewing needle bumping along. She certainly couldn't think like a sewing machine. But she was going along with the motions. And looking just as foolish as everyone else.

In the hall after class, Annie saw Michael talking to Rita in front of her locker. Annie pretended not to see them, but her heart jumped about wildly in her chest. She hurried on.

As soon as she had passed them, though, she felt a tap on her shoulder. It was Michael.

"Hi. How are you?" he asked, making sure he faced her directly.

"Okay," Annie answered, her eyes darting toward Rita, who remained at her locker, glaring. She was obviously puzzled that Michael was stopping to talk to Annie.

"I set up a time to interview your resource teacher," Michael told Annie. "I think...good article. Thanks for the idea. See you later. Bye."

It was nice of him to stop and thank me, Annie thought. But now she dreaded going to biology more than ever. What would Rita do next?

The minute Annie stepped into class, Mr. Tillis called both Rita and Annie to the back of the room.

"I understand...trouble with you girls," he said.

"Oh, no! Where'd...get...idea like that!" Rita cried. She looked straight into Mr. Tillis's eyes and smiled coyly, the way she smiled at the boys around her in class.

"...not helping her, and...not doing...Rita, like I..." he continued.

"You must have misunderstood, Mr. Tillis," Rita said. "...everything really...fine."

72

Annie stood, stunned. What could she say? How could she keep up with this slick, fast-talking girl? She couldn't even catch half of what Mr. Tillis was saying, so how could she answer anything at all!

"...complaints...some other parents..." Mr. Tillis said.

Suddenly, unable to control herself, Annie burst out, "Yes it's true! Her mother..."

"Don't be silly," Rita laughed. "I'm bending over backwards to help her...if her work...not done...not my fault."

Now Annie couldn't choke out another sound. She didn't have a chance. It seemed certain that Rita thought Annie couldn't hear or understand anything. Annie knew that people sometimes used the words *stone deaf*. Rita's mother had used the word *brick*. That's what they both thought—that Annie was just a stone or a brick. So Rita stood there calmly and lied.

Fury raged through Annie. Maybe today was the day that she would tell Ms. Gordon the whole story. Maybe it didn't matter any more what might happen if she snitched.

During lunch, Annie and Carlotta headed for the politics club lunch meeting. Annie was glad to be with Carlotta, and now she was glad that she was going to be with Bets too. Having two friends didn't take away her ache, but it helped a little.

At the front of the room, Bets was taping up a sign:

Eldorado High Welcomes Senator Gleason!

The students began to take their seats and eat their bag lunches. By the time Annie had finished hers, about fifteen seats were filled.

The senator was supposed to arrive at noon, but at ten minutes after there was still no sign of him. Anxiously, Bets checked the hall. By a quarter after, people started clapping their hands and stamping their feet.

Bets walked back and forth, checking the hall every minute. Annie felt nervous for her. Bets was always in charge and always in control of everything around her. But this time, she didn't know what to do.

"I bet he's not going to come," Carlotta said to Annie.

"He has to," Annie answered, crossing her fingers. "He just has to."

The students became more restless. A few boys started tossing empty lunch bags back and forth. Heather, a girl in Annie's art class, took off her shoes and put her feet up on the desk.

Annie felt terrible for Bets. Finally, she got up and went over to her.

"Don't worry," Annie said. "He'll be here. You did everything you could to make it work out. It's not your fault if someone else is late."

Bets squeezed Annie's hand. "I'm so glad you understand," she said.

At last a report came that the senator was on his way. Herma's brother, Mark, saw him coming down the hall and made a quick announcement to the room.

"He's coming, he's coming," Bets shrieked. "Now everyone, cool it. Pleeeeese!"

Senator Earl Gleason swept into the room in a royal manner. Michael Hale sneaked in quietly behind him and took an aisle seat next to Annie's. He smiled at her, then opened his notebook to take notes on the speech.

The senator stood near the front blackboard while Bets introduced him. "Our speaker today needs no introduction...special man who was elected to the state senate last year. We are honored...time out of his busy day.... With no further delay, I present to you Senator Earl Gleason."

Annie applauded along with everyone else.

The nice-looking blond man stepped forward and grinned for nearly a full minute before he said anything. At least that's what Annie thought because she didn't hear or see any words. Meanwhile, Bets had turned to Annie and sighed to show her relief that he had actually shown up.

"It's a pleasure to be..." the senator finally began, speaking in a loud, distinct voice. "...sorry...late, but a funny thing happened to me this morning on the way to the capitol." He laughed, and the class laughed with him. Annie missed the joke, but she laughed anyway. She didn't want to appear rude.

"...just kidding," the senator said. "While I was stuck in traffic, I tried to think of a funny story to start, but...not able to come up with a darn thing."

There was more laughter.

"Anyway," he went on, "...talk about careers in government. It's a big wide open field.... How many... think you might be interested?"

Not one hand went up. Annie saw Bets hide her head on her desk. Bets had worked so hard planning this meeting, and so far everything was going wrong. Slowly, Annie raised her hand. She hoped it would help. She also hoped desperately that the senator wouldn't ask her any questions. That could really mean disaster.

Out of the corner of her eye, she saw that Michael

appeared startled at her sudden new career claim. Now he must think she was really odd.

Senator Gleason said something, but Annie didn't catch any of it. Her heart was racing for fear that whatever it was might embarrass her—or Bets. But the senator continued. He said that politics was an exciting business, but that it took "time and guts." Then, he went on to discuss government job opportunities. It wasn't hard for Annie to catch most of his speech because he spoke clearly and expressively and used body language. He was almost an actor. Mr. Silver had told Annie's class at Sandhurst that everyone in politics was an actor.

At the end of the short speech, the senator said he only had time for three questions.

"Can you repeat what you said about summer jobs for seniors?" someone asked, and the senator repeated names and addresses the students could write to for information.

Hands shot up for the two remaining questions, and everyone shouted on top of one another. It was impossible for Annie to understand anything.

The senator looked at his watch and said, "Oops...so late...sorry, can't take your last questions ...must run. Thanks...don't forget your continued support. Tell your parents...don't forget to mention my name...."

He shook Bets's hand good-bye and off he went.

Bets leaned against the blackboard, dazed.

"Isn't he wonderful?" she sighed. "Didn't I tell you?"

Michael appeared at their side. "Short talk," he said. "Very short talk."

"But wasn't he fabulous?" Bets asked.

Annie thought that Senator Earl Gleason was okay

looking, but not fabulous. She nodded in agreement with Bets, anyway. She started to help Bets take down the welcome sign, but Michael took hold of both her shoulders and turned her toward him.

"So you...in politics?" he asked.

"No, I was trying to be polite," she answered.

"I think it might be interesting," he shrugged. "Anyway, I wondered if you would like to come to watch a district tennis tournament?" he asked.

Is this an invitation? Annie wondered. *A real invitation? Could I have misunderstood?*

"What?" she asked, to be sure.

Michael repeated what Annie thought she'd heard the first time. He told her when it started and that he really hoped she would come.

"Maybe I will," Annie answered. Maybe she really would.

CHAPTER ELEVEN

"...nnie!"

Carlotta caught Annie outside of the library and placed her open palm at her temple, the sign for *hi*, which Annie had taught her.

Annie signed *hi* back.

"Do you want to come to Tracy's house?" Carlotta began. "She bought...new tapes."

Annie didn't know any music groups or singers. Listening to music was neither easy nor fun for her. She just shrugged.

"Don't you know the...?" Carlotta asked.

Annie figured that Carlotta had mentioned the name of a group or a singer. Carlotta meant well, and Annie knew that it was hard for a hearing person to understand the everyday problems of the deaf. Even if Annie knew some of the music stars, she wouldn't be able to spend an afternoon listening to music. It wasn't part of her life the way it was for all these kids around her. And it never could be.

Annie explained that she was on her way to re-source, and she waved good-bye and smiled as she headed off.

She found Ms. Gordon hunched over her desk with her nose almost touching the book she was reading.

She didn't look up until Annie sat down and said *hello*. Then Ms. Gordon stuck a straw from a juice carton in her book as a bookmark and gave Annie her full attention.

"I want to change out of my biology class," Annie signed.

Ms. Gordon breathed deeply and twisted her mouth, thinking. "Have you tried your best?" she signed.

"Yes."

"Doesn't Mr. Tillis help you at all?"

"Not very much, but he's not the only problem in that class," Annie finally admitted. "Everyone at my table is a problem, too. Every day they make me want to disappear."

"I'm so sorry to hear that's been happening. Would an assignment at a different table make it better?" Ms. Gordon asked and signed.

Annie shook her head.

Ms. Gordon twisted her mouth thoughtfully again. "I'll see what I can do to change your class," she told Annie.

Annie remembered the boy who had fallen off the skateboard in the park. And how she had told him it was okay to cry because it was foolish to force yourself to be brave when you didn't feel like it. Right now Annie felt like a coward, and she let her eyes well up with tears.

Ms. Gordon came around from her desk and put her arm around Annie.

Annie touched her fingertips to her lips to say *thank you*.

At the end of the day, Annie realized that she had left her biology report in the classroom. She had worked hard on it. A full week. Hopefully, the door would not be locked. She could simply retrieve it before it was thrown into the garbage.

The door wasn't locked, but, as soon as she stepped into the room, she saw Rita, Brad, and Taylor. There was another boy, too, poking around a microscope, but he didn't look up the way the others did.

Annie swallowed hard and headed straight for her place at the table. *Keep your eyes front and head up straight,* she told herself. *Eyes front, head straight. Maybe next week I'll be in another class. Maybe I'll never have to bother with these people again.*

Where's my report? she wondered. She just wanted to get it and leave. But it wasn't where she'd left it. Then she spotted it. Taylor had rolled it up into a cylinder, and he was tapping it on Rita's knees.

"Pl...pl...ease. That's mine," Annie said, pushing the words out nervously.

"This?" Taylor held up the paper and waved it around over his head.

"Yes," she managed to breathe.

Taylor smirked and tossed it up toward the ceiling. Brad caught it and tossed it up again.

Annie stood limply. The noises and faces blurred before her. She reached a trembling hand out in one last plea for what belonged to her. The boys started to play catch with it.

The boy at the microscope moved forward and joined the group. They all started talking and laughing as if Annie couldn't hear a word. As if she didn't have feelings. As if she were actually a stone.

In the midst of this she found herself picking up words like "break-in...so simple you wouldn't believe...soon as it gets dark...tomorrow night... chicken...deaf and can't hear a thing...keep the principal guessing...until dark...."

At last, Taylor let Annie's report fall to the floor. They all watched as she stumbled forward to pick it up and run from the room.

In the hall, Annie shook with humiliation. She had made the request to change out of that class not a day too soon.

Suddenly she realized what she had just heard. *Could I have heard right?* she wondered. *Was it real? Were they really planning to break in some place? Vandalize the school? Was that it? And if that's what they planned, when? Tomorrow night?*

It seemed crazy. But it made sense—it really did. The secrets, the missing things at school, their awful behavior. They were planning something terrible. And they thought she didn't know a thing about it.

CHAPTER TWELVE

Annie was deeply relieved the next day to learn that she didn't have to go to Mr. Tillis's biology class any more. Ms. Gordon had rearranged her schedule so that she had art earlier and a different science class after lunch. The new class had a nice teacher and also a student teacher, who was especially helpful to Annie.

But all that day a bad feeling tugged at Annie. She sensed that something bad was going to happen. And soon.

Annie remembered a story that Kay had told her. Kay had an uncle who was scheduled to fly from Sacramento to Washington early one morning. He woke that day in a sweat. He sensed that something was going to happen to his flight so he cancelled his reservation. And sure enough, that plane actually crashed, and there were no survivors. Everyone asked him how he knew, and he said he couldn't really answer. It was something that he just felt.

That was how Annie felt now. It was uncomfortable, too, carrying a secret like this. She wanted desperately to tell someone. But people would probably think she was crazy. Even Bets and Carlotta.

All the way home from school, Annie tried to forget

about her thoughts. But she couldn't. She sat in the crowded kitchen, folding laundry and stacking it on the table, wondering why the situation was bothering her so much. Why was she so concerned, anyway?

Was it because she hated those kids from her old biology table so much that she wanted to see them punished? What if it were other kids she had over-heard making such unthinkable plans? People who were nicer to her, or people she didn't know? Would it bother her so much then?

Annie put away the stacks of clothing and went into the bathroom to wash her hair. She stood for a long time in front of the mirror, making faces and smiling different smiles. Suddenly, she found herself imagining being with Michael Hale after the tennis tournament he had mentioned. He was in his tennis whites, and she was wearing a brightly colored Mexican skirt and an off-the-shoulder blouse. They were strolling together in the dark with no other peo-ple in sight. Then he turned to her, reached out, and touched her cheek. He did not speak. He didn't need to. His eyes told her how much he cared about her.

Ouch! She had let the hot hair dryer accidentally touch her neck. She turned it off and shook her nearly dry hair so that it hung loose and fluffy. After that, she wandered restlessly about the apartment until Gil came home.

"What's for dinner?" Gil asked, rolling his eyes and rubbing his stomach.

"An *anything* dinner," Annie answered. That meant there wasn't much in the refrigerator, and Gil and Annie could put together anything they could find. Their father was working that night.

Gil grumbled.

"Will you call Kay's house for me?" Annie asked.

"And ask her mother to ask Kay if she can visit for another weekend. And how soon." Annie wished she could talk to Kay right now and tell her what was on her mind. Kay would be the only person who wouldn't accuse her of being crazy or letting her imagination run wild. Especially when she reminded Kay about her uncle.

Gil agreed to call, and he dialed on the kitchen phone. Annie couldn't read his lips because they were so close to the phone mouthpiece. It was a brief conversation, and afterward Gil told Annie that Kay's mother was planning to invite Annie to visit during winter vacation. One of Kay's sisters was going to be away for a few days, and Annie could sleep in her bed.

Annie clasped her hands excitedly. It seemed a long time until winter vacation, but how wonderful it would be to go back! How wonderful to see Kay and everyone at Sandhurst! They all meant so much to her. The whole deaf community did. That was Annie's first world, and she never wanted to lose it.

Annie and Gil put together their *anything* dinners. They found leftover vegetable soup, wheat crackers, cheddar cheese chunks, frozen ravioli, and the last of a batch of brownies that Annie had baked.

"Gil?" Annie asked as they started to clear the table. She thought she might mention the school situation that was bothering her and maybe get some advice from him.

He looked up, ready to answer, but she changed her mind. He would only tease her. "Nothing," she shrugged. Instead she asked if he were planning to stay home that night.

"I'm going out for a few hours," he told her. "Do you want me to call a friend for you?"

"No thanks."

"Sure?"

Annie nodded and watched him throw his sweats into a bag and leave. She settled in front of the TV set and watched an old "I Love Lucy" show. It was hard to believe that Lucy was no longer alive to make those expressive faces and to entertain in that wonderful way she had. Sometimes it was even harder to believe that Annie's mother was not alive. Annie could have gone to her immediately, and her mother would have believed her and known exactly what to do.

Annie glanced toward the window. It was starting to get dark. She grew more uneasy by the minute. Tonight was the night those vandals were going to break into the school. She thought of the valuable antique light that Bets said she needed to guard with her life. And the typewriters and computer in Michael's newspaper office. And even though Annie didn't like Mr. Tillis, she hated to see all those expensive microscopes in his room damaged. She had finally learned how to use them correctly and see what she was supposed to see on a slide, instead of viewing only her eyelashes.

Annie realized how much she cared about the school and everything in it. No matter how hard this new world was for her, it was *her* school now. She was part of it. She cared about people at the school, too. Sure, she wanted to see the bad ones punished. But it was no longer the most important reason for her concern.

Annie knew now that it would be wrong to sit back and do nothing. She had to try in spite of what people might think of her. The problem was, who could she go to? She had no idea how to get in touch with either Ms. Gordon or Bets. Carlotta's family did not seem to be the kind of family that would want to get involved. Michael came to mind, but he would never believe anything bad about Rita.

There was only one thing left to do. Go directly to the police station. She grabbed a sweater and hurried out, locking the door behind her. At first she walked at a steady pace. A few blocks later, she broke into a run.

By the time she ran up the police station steps and opened the door, she was nearly out of breath. It was several minutes before she approached the front desk.

"...help you, Miss?" A uniformed officer asked.

"I...I...it's hard to know where to start...." Her nervousness made it hard for Annie to speak.

"What?" The officer leaned forward.

Annie tried again, but from his puzzled expression, she could tell she was not making herself understood.

"Speak up, dear....hard...speaking...." the officer interrupted.

Annie bit her lip. "I'm sure that over at the high school..." she began, but before she could go on, he picked up the telephone and turned his attention to the phone conversation. When he hung up, he asked Annie if she had a cold or sore throat.

Annie shook her head and concentrated on trying to explain herself slowly and distinctly. She managed to tell him what she thought was going to happen, and she suggested that the police stop it. But it was no use. The officer's expression turned from puzzled to annoyed. Did he think that something was really wrong with her?

"...proof?..." he finally asked.

"Not exactly, but..."

"Well, maybe you better..." he began, then bent his

head down to shuffle papers inside a desk drawer. "Listen dear," he said when he looked up again, "...come back with someone else who knows about this, okay?"

Annie slumped in defeat. There was no point standing here for one more second. Without saying another word, she turned and fled. It was only when she found herself on the corner of Westhill and Spring that it occurred to her that Michael Hale was her last hope of getting someone to understand. She didn't know which of the corner houses he lived in, so she picked one at random and rang the bell. When a woman answered, Annie asked if a boy named Michael lived there. The woman said something that Annie didn't catch, but she pointed to a two-story house across the street.

Annie hurried to the house across the street and rang the bell. No one answered. She tried again. Still no response. Annie knocked loudly, and at last a girl answered. Then an older woman appeared behind her and scolded the girl for opening the door to a stranger. The girl shouted back, telling her mother that she had asked and asked who it was but nobody had answered.

"I'm sorry," Annie apologized. "Please. Does Michael Hale live here? I need to see him."

The woman smiled and invited Annie inside.

Michael was surprised to see Annie. He noticed at once that she was upset.

"What's wrong?" he asked.

"Can we talk outside?" Annie asked in return. There was too much commotion inside.

The two of them went out and sat on the front step of the house. Annie told Michael the whole story.

"Oh, Annie, that can't be possible," Michael said when she finished. "How can you be so sure?"

This was just the response that Annie had been afraid of. She twisted the edge of her sweater in frustration.

"I knew you were going to say that," she answered, breathing hard. "But it's true."

"But, you only heard bits and pieces," he told her, "and they don't fit together. They don't make any sense. I know it's hard for you to hear everything...I know you're upset..."

"Oh, please..." Annie begged. "Don't think I'm crazy, too, like that police officer. You have to believe that I did hear right. I did understand. And I know those kids."

"Annie, Rita may not be the world's most thoughtful person, but she would never get mixed up in anything like that. She would never be involved in a crime! Anyway, I just left her a while ago."

That was like a splash of cold water in Annie's face. It was no use. She stood to leave.

"I didn't misunderstand," she said firmly. They were her last words to Michael as she turned and hurried off, never looking back at him. Block after block she ran. It was cold and dark, and she was really alone. She wanted to tell what she knew. She wanted to help. But no one would listen. No one would believe her.

When she reached the school she stopped. There was a car parked in the lot. It didn't belong to a maintenance man, either. It was a new sports car. She leaned against a tree, pressing her aching side, wondering who that car belonged to. A moment later, she saw a figure in a basement window. It had to be one of them! It had to be!

Frantic and out of breath, Annie rushed to a nearby house. When a man answered the door, all she was able to do was point to the school and mutter, "police...call."

Although he didn't know the reason, the man went to the phone and put through the call. Within minutes, a patrol car with two officers pulled up. By then, Annie had regained some of her wind, and she explained what she could.

The officers crossed the street and quietly approached the window where Annie had said she'd seen a figure. She started to follow them, but they told her to stay back for her own safety. The police crept into the building.

Minutes passed. Nothing was happening. *What if I'm mistaken, after all?* Annie suddenly wondered. *What if I did misunderstand? What if it was only my imagination? The gossip will get around school in no time. I'll look ridiculous!* She swallowed hard.

The man who had made the phone call tried to ask Annie something. But it was too dark for her to see his lips. Besides, she was too nervous to make the effort. She could only stand, shaking uncontrollably. Her pulse beat wildly.

At last, the officers came out of a side door. Three people were with them. Annie breathed deeply with relief. She had been right. She would not appear the dummy some people thought she was.

The figures came closer until Annie was finally able to see who they were—Taylor, Brad, and the other boy she had seen with them in the biology lab. Rita was not among them, but Rita had known the plan all along. Annie would bet her life on it.

The boys were furious. They lashed out and kicked. The third boy spit on the ground near Annie's feet.

They were prodded roughly to the patrol car, and as they were being shoved inside, another patrol car pulled alongside. There was a lot of fast talking on the patrol car radios.

Annie wanted to know exactly what had happened. Had the boys been caught early enough to stop them, or had they already caused a great deal of damage? But she wasn't able to learn anything. There was too much commotion to hear well and the darkness hampered her speech reading. Finally, one of the officers drove Annie home and told her that she would be contacted later.

Exhausted, Annie fell asleep on the sofa until her father and Gil returned.

The next day, everyone in homeroom was talking about the incident. Annie knew that the whole school was buzzing about the news. Annie had learned that the boys broke dozens of windows, smashed typewriters and science equipment, dumped contents out of office filing drawers, and splattered paint on walls and desks on every floor. Bets's valuable light, though, remained unharmed.

It was shocking to Annie. She had done the best she could, but she only wished that she had been able to prevent that terrible damage.

When Annie was called out of homeroom to go to the office, everyone stared and whispered. They were eager to get the inside story. They wanted to know how she had put the pieces of the strange puzzle together.

In the office, Annie found the two arresting officers, the principal, and Michael with his notepad in hand. The glass on the door was shattered, and a huge file cabinet was dumped over, with folders scattered everywhere. What a mess!

One of the officers explained Annie's role to the principal.

"I see," the principal said. "So this is the girl. who....glad you did what...sure it wasn't easy...right thing...."

Michael said something to the principal, which Annie didn't catch, and the principal and one of the officers talked hurriedly and animatedly. She didn't know what was going on with them, either. It made her angry. Why did they send for her if they were going to talk behind her back like this! Finally, she asked Michael what everyone was talking about.

Michael took Annie aside and filled her in. Then he lowered his eyes briefly before looking straight at Annie. "I'm so sorry I didn't believe you when you tried to tell me about Rita," he apologized. "I feel rotten about.... I hope you can forgive me."

"What do you mean exactly?" Annie asked.

"Rita did know," Michael said. "...like you said.... At the station, the boys had to tell every detail, and she was included in the story. She is coming down to the office now."

Annie gasped. It would not be easy for the girls to face each other.

"It's so awful," she murmured. "Why did they do it?"

"A lot of reasons, I guess, from what I understand," Michael answered. "Taylor was about to be expelled from school for cheating, and some people think he has been stealing for a long time.... Bad family trouble at home, too.... Brad had some problems, too.... drugs...."

"Is his mother on TV?" Annie asked.

"Right. Judy Snapdragon," Michael answered. "Brad's parents are divorced....mother...glamorous life...traveling all over the world.... Brad not accepted on the football team...."

"What about the other boy?" Annie asked.

"Bucky? He went along for the ride. For the fun. Some fun!"

Finally, the principal told Annie that he wanted to ask her a few questions to learn how she found out about the break-in. As she answered, he listened intently. Then from over his shoulder, Annie saw Rita Leland approaching. Annie had never seen Rita when she didn't look as if she owned the world. She looked far from that now!

The principal turned angrily to Rita and asked her several questions. With each answer she cowered more, from time to time glancing at Annie and Michael standing together.

"So you did know?" the principal shouted.

"I guess so," Rita confessed.

"What do you mean, *guess?*...did or you didn't. Yes or no?"

Rita's mouth quivered. "Yes. I thought it was a joke. They joke and fool around..."

"You like to fool around like that, too?"

"I thought it was a joke. Really!" Rita was desperate. Her eyes filled with tears. She glanced once more in Annie and Michael's direction, but quickly turned away.

The principal talked about punishment, but it wasn't clear to Annie what he was saying. Michael told her that the principal said he would have to decide how to deal with Rita. "He doesn't know what to do right now," Michael explained.

A few minutes later, Annie and Michael were excused. First class had already started, and the hall monitors were gone. Annie and Michael stood in the hall alone.

"I'm so sorry..." he began to apologize again.

Annie put her finger to his lips. "Shhh," she told him. "You don't have to say it. I know."

CHAPTER THIRTEEN

"What kind of magic does this guy Michael Hale have, anyway?" Gil signed to Annie. "I didn't think anyone could drag you to a dance!"

Annie blushed. Then she held out a blank white card. "How much do you want to pledge?" she asked both Gil and her father.

Her father took a pen from his shirt pocket while he asked Annie how long she thought she would last on the dance floor.

Annie shrugged and reminded them both that the money was not for her, but for the homeless.

Gil and her father glanced at each other. If they were teaming up again, Annie didn't mind so much this time. Their expressions showed that they were happy for her. They signed their names separately, each pledging two dollars and fifty cents an hour. Gil added that he was making a real sacrifice, since that was half his hourly wage at his community college job.

"Thanks," Annie said, putting the pledge card in the pocket of her new, short, denim skirt. She also had bought a beautiful new lipstick shade, Deep Sunset, which blended perfectly with her lilac top.

After going to check herself in the mirror one more time, she returned to the living room.

"What if he doesn't come?" she asked Gil.

"Who?"

"Don't pretend you don't know what I'm talking about," she said.

"I know," Gil rotated his closed hand over his heart to sign *sorry*. "Don't worry. He'll be here. Remember, that everything might not be perfect tonight. But it will be okay. The tennis tournament you went to turned out fine, didn't it?"

"I was just watching, though," Annie explained.

"I bet Michael was flattered you were watching," Gil told her.

Annie started to make the sign for *nervous*, but Gil caught her hands. "I know you are," he said. "I would be, too."

"You would?" she asked.

He nodded.

"But, what if..."

"No more *what ifs*," Gil said. "Someone's at the door."

"Really? You mean he's here?" Annie clamped her hands to her throat. "Will you answer the door?"

"You open it," Gil urged, stepping back. Slowly Annie went to the door and opened it.

"Hi," Michael said. "You look really nice." Annie blushed again.

Gil and her father came to the doorway, and Annie introduced them to Michael.

"Enjoy the evening," Annie's father said.

"That goes double for me," Gil added.

"Ready?" Michael asked Annie. Annie took a deep breath and nodded.

The car they squeezed into held six other people. The others were talking and singing along with music on the radio. The noise was not easy to get used to, but for Annie it felt good to be with the group. She thought of Kay and how amazed she would be if she could see Annie now. Annie was going to tell her all the details and how something can be scary and fun at the same time.

Inside the gym, one of the girls from Annie's P.E. class remarked that it was hard to believe this was the same place where they had become the heart and soul of a machine. Annie laughed. *It's true*, Annie thought. She'd helped Bets transform the gym into a 1920's dance hall. They'd done quite a job!

Bets's antique light was rotating slowly from the center of the ceiling, flashing reflections all around the room. Nearly every inch of wall was covered with decorations and trim. From the doorway, Annie could see Bets up on the stage; she was directing people the way she always did. Right next to the band, was a portable blackboard. On it was written:

Thanks to Super Fried Chicken for the
chicken wing contributions and the
Midtown Mart for the discount on
drinks and ice cream.

Bets took a piece of chalk and printed in big letters:

Hour One

Annie stepped further into the gym. The music was blaring so loudly that she turned her hearing aids down.

Someone caught her and Michael and showed them where to sign their names and the time they started dancing and told them the rules. Annie didn't understand the rules, but Michael explained them to her afterward. He was in a hurry to start dancing.

"Can't I watch first?" she asked him.

"No, that's a rule—no watching first," he laughed. "Come on, all you have to do is stand with me...move a^ arm or hip every five seconds."

It didn't sound so hard the way Michael put it. She let him lead her onto the floor. Immediately he started twisting and bending and rocking. Annie watched, and then she began to slide her feet back and forth, swivel her hips, twist, and bend a little. The music was loud and she felt the vibrations through the wooden floor.

Michael smiled and nodded, then reached his hand out for hers.

"...no rules against...." he said.

"Sorry. What?" Annie asked.

Michael leaned closer and moved his lips slowly. "There are no rules against touching," he said.

Annie tingled at his touch. And slowly, she began to move to the beat of the music.

DATE DUE

10/20/94		
Apr. 2		
A̶p̶r̶		
May		